DYING *For A*
SECOND
CHANCE

A PSYCHOLOGICAL THRILLER

JENN CHAPMAN

DYING *For A*
SECOND
CHANCE

JENN CHAPMAN

woodhall press

Woodhall Press | Norwalk, CT

woodhall press

Woodhall Press, 81 Old Saugatuck Road, Norwalk, CT 06855
WoodhallPress.com

Cover design: GetCovers.com
Layout artist: L.J. Mucci

Library of Congress Cataloging-in-Publication Data available

ISBN 978-1-960456-00-7   (paper: alk paper)
ISBN 978-1-960456-01-4   (electronic)

First Edition
Distributed by Independent Publishers Group
(800) 888-4741

Printed in the United States of America

This is a work of fiction. Names, characters, business, events and inci-
dents are the products of the author's imagination. Any resemblance
to actual persons, living or dead, or actual events is purely coincidental.

This book is dedicated to my mother, Marylou, who instilled several virtues in me that I draw on to this day – perseverance, patience, and forgiveness. And to my father, Dave, who encouraged me to never give up on my dream of sharing my writing. It was he, when I was three, who sat on the step comforting me when I accidentally jabbed a pencil in the palm of my hand, forever branding me as a writer!

PREFACE

Well-being in most Indigenous communities includes the overlapping relationship between humans and forces in the spirit world. Generally, this blending of dimensions respects a permeable boundary which organizes the seen, physical human world on one side and the unseen spirits on the other. In many Indigenous cultures, it is also a normal interface for a spirit force to manifest itself in a human body.

(Braden 2008, Emoto 2004, Parry 2006).

"Rid yourselves of all the offenses you have committed, and get a new heart and a new spirit...For I take no pleasure in the spiritual death of anyone, declares the Sovereign Lord."

Old Testament, New International version, Ezekiel 18:31-32

"What good will it be for a man if he gains the whole world, yet forfeits his soul? Or what can a man give in exchange for his soul?"

New Testament, New International version, Matthew 16:26

"It is God that takes the souls (of men) at death; and those that die not (He takes) during their sleep: those on whom He has passed the decree of death, He keeps back (from returning to life), but the rest He sends (to their bodies) for a term appointed, verily in this are Signs for those who reflect."

Qur'an 39:42

"*In the world of spirit there is no retrogression. The world of mortality is a world of contradictions, of opposites; motion being compulsory everything must either go forward or retreat. In the realm of spirit there is no retreat possible, all movement is bound to be towards a perfect state. 'Progress' is the expression of spirit in the world of matter. The intelligence of man, his reasoning powers, his knowledge, his scientific achievements, all these being manifestations of the spirit, partake of the inevitable law of spiritual progress and are, therefore, of necessity, immortal.*"

– 'Abdu'l-Bahá, *Paris Talks*

CHAPTER ONE

Marie

"KIND PEOPLE ARE MY KINDA PEOPLE" the sign in front of the yoga studio read, as I drove by on that lightning-filled night. In the downpour, the rain flash-flooded the road, coming down in sheets as though someone had unzipped the clouds and the water just fell, thunk.

Kind people are my kind of people...That's certainly true, I thought. *Does anyone ever intentionally spend their time with unkind people?* I wondered what cute message would be written on the other side of the sign. Glancing in the side mirror I was blinded by headlights as a large truck T-boned my little Toyota, sending it in whirling circles. The impact whipped me back against the headrest as the airbag punched me in the face. The wrenching noise of the crash turned from a screeching cacophony to a scraping rasp as the car settled itself against a tree. I felt myself slipping away. How will they ever get me out of here, I thought, and then I was out, standing in front of the car. Only my body wasn't...my poor broken body was still slumped on the seat. I checked out the scene, like I was watching a movie. Heather was strapped tightly, in her car seat in the back, screaming for me. The man driving the truck had gotten out, limped around and opened the passenger door, where his wife was trapped by a tree branch that had been sheared off by my car. Hurtling through the air, it had speared its way through the truck window. A fork in its limbs was pinning her, on both sides of her neck, to the seat. I watched as he checked her pulse, then pulled out his phone, and made the 911 call. Slumped over, sobbing, his hands resting on his knees, he cried for her, "Jessie, Jessie!" He didn't see her outside the truck. Like me, she was in two places.

I watched, mesmerized, as she came over to my car, looked in at Heather, then tried to open the door. *"You can't,"* I said to her with my thoughts. *"I tried."* She turned and smiled at me. Her spirit began to change form. Losing her humanness, she became a light being, growing larger, moving into the mist, finally fading into the rain that didn't touch her. Wistfully, I wondered if it would be like that for me too, as I moved from this world into the next.

Oh my God! I'm dead! The dreamlike watching turned into dread and panic. *Heather! I'm all that little girl has. Who will take care of her?* My mind screamed, like her cries, like the ambulance siren as it traveled through the streets, coming too late for me.

The man from the truck crossed to my car. As he stepped into the glare from the headlights I wished to God I had left with his wife's spirit because I knew him. James. He worked at a gas station in the town where I had lived before, always flirting with the girl customers. I was flattered that he chose me, one day, to ask out for dinner. I met him that night. Big mistake. All he talked about were the other women he had met at the station, how none of them were "right" for him, and how he rarely went out with anyone twice. When I got home I found out why. He had followed me. As I stepped into the house, he came out of the shadow of a hemlock tree, pushed his way in, and raped me on my polished oak floor.

I never got gas at that station again. After the rape, afraid he would come back to my house, I returned home to my mother. I curled up inside me, like the baby waiting in my womb. As I grew bigger during my pregnancy, my shame grew too, because I had not reported it. My mother didn't believe I had been raped by someone I went out with willingly, so why would anyone else, she said. My mother wasn't kind. She was mean-spirited and cruel. I watched other mothers with their children while I was growing up and never witnessed the abusive behavior that tore apart my heart. So, I figured it was my fault. There was something wrong with me that brought out the meanness in her.

I knew better when I had my own child, Heather. She saw my mother for who she was, and never went near her. If we were visiting and I had to use the bathroom, Heather would crawl down the hall, lie on the floor, and peek under the door, making sure I was still there and hadn't left her alone with the scary grandmother.

When my mother died last month, I left our town and all its bad memories. Moving several miles down the coast didn't seem very far, but for me it was as though I had traveled to another country. In a way, I had. Tokeland is a tiny, drive-by town, on the edge of the continent near the Pacific Ocean, in Washington. It borders the Shoalwater Bay Reservation. I worked remotely, as a medical coder both for the Shoalwater Tribe, and for a small clinic in Aberdeen. I was fortunate to have work where I could be home with my daughter in our tiny apartment.

That night we had been at the Tribal Center where I played Bingo. Heather, worn out from all the old grandmas playing with her, was curled up in her car seat with her blanket, sleeping soundly, until I crashed the car.

Next to my car, I watched James look at my body, and I wondered if he recognized me. He strained to look into the back seat, to see

3

who was crying. Going around to the other side, he opened the door, and unstrapped her car seat. I watched, horror-struck, as he carried her to his truck and strapped her in. *He is stealing my baby! Dear God, no! Please help me. Why does he want her? That child is mine, he can't take her!*

I watched as he came back to my car and took the insurance card and the spare house key from my purse. *Can souls collapse? Am I going to melt onto the pavement, becoming one with the rain in a puddle of tears?*

The police and ambulance arrived. He told them he thinks his wife is gone, but that I might be alive. They found my lifeless body in the car. He said he had a child in the truck, and they went to check on her. *"Liar!"* I jumped in front of him, waving my arms. I wanted to tear him apart but I couldn't make him see me or hear me.

One of the medics had removed Heather and was checking her vitals in the ambulance. I moved closer to the truck as another medic worked on his wife, giving her CPR.

I knew her spirit had left. There was no way she could be revived. In a desperate act, I prayed with all my soul, *"Please, God, Jesus, Buddha, Universe...if there is anyone out there listening, please let her live...let me live in her...let me be her... let me raise my baby!"* I was immediately connected to her, and the most unimaginable pain in her head, as I heard the paramedic say, "She has a pulse!"

CHAPTER TWO

Jimmy

I couldn't believe it when I saw Marie dead, in that torn-up car. The last time I saw her she was on the floor in her living room, crying. She didn't know how lucky she was to be lying there alive. She should have been dead. The rope was in my pocket. But when she begged me to stop, said that she could get pregnant, my mind grabbed onto that thought and I refused to kill her. I've always wanted a kid of my own. What if she did get pregnant? We could start over. She could get to know the nice me, the guy who didn't behave like that. I kept obsessing on the idea. I covered her up with a blanket and left the house.

A few days later, when I realized what I had done — left a witness who could identify me as a rapist — I went back. The landlady was there cleaning. She didn't know anything, except that Marie had moved back in with her mother, somewhere in another town. I never saw her again until tonight.

I moved away too, and got another job. I hoped she would just let it all go. I lived in fear that the police would show up at my door. Around six months later I stopped being scared.

I started going out and watching people again. That's when I met Jessica. She was a waitress in a diner just off the highway. She handled the truck drivers really well; nicely, but firm. She didn't take any shit from no one. She was funny too; made me laugh every time I went in there. I didn't ask her out.

One night in November, on her dinner break, she came to my table. "Hey, sugar! Mind if I join you?" she asked, and sat down across from me. "So, I was in the grocery store today. A lady was picking through the frozen turkeys for Thanksgiving, but she couldn't find one big enough for her family. She asked a stock boy, 'Do these turkeys get any bigger?' The stock boy replied, 'No ma'am, they're dead.' ...That's a joke, Jimmy. That didn't really happen. But I did buy a turkey. I love to cook Thanksgiving dinner with all the trimmings. And I'm inviting you to come to dinner." That's how we started going out. She asked me.

By Christmas, we had been to a football game, gone fishing with a friend of hers in Westport, and took the ferry to Seattle to ride the Ferris wheel and the carousel, and to shop at Pike Place Market. I had never done any of these things. It felt strange, but good, to be seen as a normal person living a normal life. That's when I started thinking again about being a father. I knew she would be a good mother, watching her in the diner with other people's kids. So, I told her that, and asked her to marry me.

She cried. "I can't have any kids, Jimmy. I had to have a hysterectomy three years ago."

"So, marry me anyway and we'll adopt," I told her. We got married in February.

And now it's almost Easter, and I'm going through Marie's apartment looking for a birth certificate for that little baby they took to the hospital. I'm sure that kid's mine, and I need proof, 'cause there is no way in hell the doctors will believe it's Jessie's if they get a look inside her. I rummage through the desk until I find a folder with the birth certificate.

Heather Lily Harper. 10/14/2017. Mother: Marie Rose Harper. Father: Unknown. Born at Aberdeen General Hospital. A girl. Born in October. That would make her pregnant in January. Bingo.

I packed up all the stuff I could find of Heather's, including the crib, and put it in my truck. The dent on the front right fender and the hole in the window were the only evidence of the accident that took my baby's mother's life. What are the odds that we would both move to Tokeland, that she would live three blocks from me, and that I would kill her? Kill her accidentally, not on purpose like I almost did before. What are the chances I would get a baby for Jessie and me to raise...my very own baby?

CHAPTER THREE

Rod

Sergeant Rodney Kills On Top leaned back against the tree and took a long drink of cold coffee. Bark had been scraped from the trunk by the crashing car, and the scent of cedar pitch filled his nostrils. Eyes closed, he imagined he was in the sweat lodge with vapors from the cedar-scented steam spilling over him. He stroked the tree trunk with his free hand, like he had caressed the baby's head before the paramedics took her and the woman away. So much damage to so many people from one tree on a rainy night. It took them forever to get Jessica Wilson freed from the truck seat so they could transport her. With that tree branch trapping her by the neck, they had to cut through the seat and saw the limb off, leaving a small twig in her throat. He couldn't believe she lived through that. The woman driving the car, Marie Harper, never knew what happened, thankfully. The impact of the crash tore her door off, crushed her against the tree, severing her at the waist. Jimmy Wilson, the driver of the truck, had given Rod all the information about what had happened, and checked with him to make sure it was all right to leave the scene. It was clearly Marie Harper's fault. She ran the stop sign. The car was registered in Hoquiam. Judging by the address Marie had written on the back of her license, she lived out here, now, on the edge of the reservation. Maybe she hadn't driven on this street before. Maybe in the storm she didn't see the stop sign. Maybe, maybe, maybe...now she's dead. He hated this part of his job.

He finished his coffee then took her keys and purse from the Toyota, before the tow truck hooked up. He checked the back seat for anything, and found a small baby sock and a pacifier on the floor. He threw them in the purse, got in his car and headed to the hospital to get details he needed to finish the accident report.

As he drove the two-lane highway through the forest, along the bay, and into Aberdeen, Rod wondered what his life would be like if he had stayed in North Dakota. It had been harsh, growing up on the Fort Berthold Reservation. His grandparents' generation was the last of the farmers, growing beans, corn and squash on the fertile land next to the Missouri River. They had lived at peace with their white neighbors, farmers all. Then, in the 1950s, the Garrison Dam was built by the Army Corp of Engineers, a project meant to better the lives of many...but not his people. They lost their land, homes, ranches and the only medical clinic. The river had been a means of transportation, canoeing across to visit families that lived on the other side. After the dam was built there was a lake, too big for a canoe to cross. The promised bridge was never built, forcing them to drive more than sixty miles to visit their family for Sunday dinner.

Rod had been raised by his grandmother, mostly. The reservation was a stretch of land almost a million acres in size, the belly of which held the badlands. Lewis and Clark went through there and got Sacagawea, the gifted guide who made the rest of their journey possible. Because the land was so inhospitable to the white people, the Mandan, Hidatsa and Arikara people were left alone, never made to move. No "Trail of Tears" for them, just a lifetime of tears.

After barely making it out of his teen years alive, Rod had joined his sister, Samantha, who had moved to Washington to go to medical school. Now she's the tribal doctor for the Shoalwater people. He had gone to the academy, joined the reservation police force, and worked his way up to patrol sergeant. He took a lot of guff over his name, Kills On Top, being a cop. Tonight, he was called out because of the fatality. Now he had to go into Aberdeen, to the hospital, and finish it.

He pulled into the hospital parking lot and hurried in through the rain. He stood in the lobby, shaking the water off of him like a big dog, then checked at the front desk. He learned that Jessica Wilson had been taken to surgery, and the baby to the Pediatric Ward. He wandered down there and spoke to Daniel, the nurse in charge.

"I'm Sergeant Kills On Top. Has Jimmy Wilson, the baby's father, come in yet? He didn't give us any information at the scene about the baby. I don't even know its name. Is it OK?"

"It is a 'she' and yes, she seems fine. Want to take a peek?" They went into her room where she lay asleep, sucking on a pacifier.

"She's been here over two hours and the dad still hasn't shown up. I hope he's all right," Daniel worried.

"He said something about going back to the house to get some of the baby's things. I'm sure he'll be along soon," shared Rod.

"Well, I hope he brings her formula. Some babies are on special formula because they can't digest milk and we need to know."

"I'm going to the police station to fill out my report and find next-of-kin for the dead woman," said Rod. "When Jimmy arrives, please tell him I'll be back soon."

CHAPTER FOUR

Jimmy returned home and unloaded the truck, putting all the baby's things in the guest room, as though they had always been there. After he took a shower, he put his blood-soaked clothes in the washer. As he watched his wife's blood run from his shirt into the soapy water, he flashed back to the last time he had done this very same thing, three months ago. Only then he wasn't married. Only then it was another woman's blood. He had taken her to dinner at his usual spot, then back to his place for a drink. His garage floor was James's recreational space. He had choked her so hard the clothesline cut her flesh like a knife, pouring her life out into his lap. That had been a hard one to clean up. After he finished with her, he stuffed her in large, black lawn bags, put her in the back of his truck, drove out to the reservation, and dumped her in the woods.

As the washer started to agitate, it pulled him back to the present. He was hungry, and only then did he think about baby food. He had forgotten to look for that in Marie's kitchen! Do babies even eat food at that age? Did Marie nurse her, or does she drink from a bottle? He couldn't go back, he had to get to the hospital. How was he going to manage this huge lie? He grabbed a Coke out of the fridge and made himself a peanut butter sandwich. After covering the hole in his windshield with clear plastic, he got in his truck and headed back to town, to the hospital.

Meanwhile, Rod drove down the winding road where the hospital perched behind him on top of the hill. Across town, in the police station he settled into the cubicle he shared with Carmen Sandoval, his partner of the last four years. Their space was small, carved out at the back of the office, in between the copy machine and the lunchroom. Boxes of material they had collected as they worked a serial murder case were stacked between their desks. Four women, all raped and strangled, all dumped on the reservation, and no clues as yet. The FBI was in charge since it was federal, and they had loaned Carmen to the Aberdeen Police Department to investigate the case. Rod was on loan too, from the Shoalwater Tribal Police. He was so glad to have her expertise, as well as a new friend. She was working late, at her computer. "What's up Kemosabe?"

He snorted at the reference, and threw her a cookie left from his drive-through dinner. She caught it, put it between her teeth, and continued to type, her short black hair with the pink tips bobbing along to the music coming through her earbuds.

"I just came from the hospital. I stopped here to write up a traffic accident that happened tonight out on the rez. It's a fatality." He dropped the purse he had picked up from Marie's car onto the table, opened it up, took out her ID, and sat at his computer. As the purse tipped over, Carmen grabbed it before everything spilled to the floor. She picked up the pacifier and sock. "Hijole...was there a kid in the accident?" she asked. "Yeah, in the truck that hit this lady's car. She was ok. They took her to the hospital." "Huh," she said, twirling the sock on her finger. "Looks like this woman has one too. Wonder where it is? Is there a husband you can call?" She grabbed Marie's phone out of the purse. It wasn't locked. She checked the contacts page. "She's got two medical clinic numbers listed, a real estate rental agency, a pediatrician, and a couple of women, that's all. So, she must have a kid. Just no husband. Maybe she's got a wife?"

Rod took the sock, looked at the size, thought a minute, and grabbed the purse and its contents. "I'll be back," he said as he hurried out of the office. He drove back to the hospital wondering why he got these sixth sense kind of feelings. He knew something was wrong. Whenever he had these powerful nudges and he didn't follow through, things went bad. Like the day the boys drowned. Before he was twelve, Rod had lost three small cousins who were riding their sled late one afternoon near the lagoons on the edge of town. Searchers found the tracks and the hole in the ice just as it was getting dark. The next morning, they went back and were able to find the bodies in the pond. The police had questioned him and every other boy in the neighborhood because they had found larger boot tracks, as though someone had been pulling the smaller boys through the snow. He had never admitted to being there. One minute he was giving them a ride, and the next they had all disappeared, the rope slipping through his hands, following them into the icy water. His gut told him he shouldn't pull them out on the ice, but they begged him to push them, and let them slide across. Only they didn't slide, they fell. He had carried the guilt and remorse every moment since. He had the same intuitive feeling today. Something was niggling him to check out this baby.

Just as he entered the pediatric ward, the on-call doctor came in and introduced herself to Rod, who gave her his card. "We have a problem here, Sergeant. We did blood work on both the baby and the mother. The baby's blood type does not match Jessica Wilson's. She can't be her mother!"

Rod stood with his hands in his pockets, mulling that over. What was Occam's Razor Theory about problem-solving — the simplest explanation is probably the right one? If Jessica isn't the mother, maybe they adopted it. Maybe they were babysitting someone else's kid, or maybe... It belonged to Marie Harper! He opened her purse, took out the pacifier and the sock, and gave them to Dr. Ford. "If I were you, I'd be checking the blood type of the dead woman," he said. "I'm going back out to her place to see what I can find. Please call me if you learn anything."

CHAPTER FIVE

Rod headed back out to Tokeland, intent on searching Marie's place for anything that might help him understand what was going on, and to see if he could find information on next-of-kin. As he came around the curve just before the Westport Winery, two ambulances whizzed past, heading back toward Aberdeen. He saw flashing lights ahead, slowed down, and pulled over. It looked like someone had tried to pass on the curve and hit an oncoming car head-on. He got out to see if the state patrolman needed assistance. He didn't, the ambulances had left and he was waiting for the tow trucks. Luckily there were no fatalities. Rod noticed that both cars reeked of alcohol.

As he continued his drive, he thought back to the year he turned fifteen, the year his father was killed in a head-on accident, hit by a drunk driver. His dad was sober, and had been for two years. The irony was, it was his dad's best friend, George, who crashed into him. George could have used that as a wake-up call, but did he? Nah. He just kept on drinking until one winter night when he went out into a

17

30-below snowstorm, took a wrong turn to the outhouse and froze to death. They found him standing with his pants down, leaning on a tree.

Rod had been drunk once, knew it was his doom, and stopped. He always remembered what that white teacher had said to them, one day in class. She was the specialist hired to work with the Gifted and Talented Program. She had convinced the superintendent that they were all gifted in some way, and the arts were the way to showcase that, so she started a drama class for high school students. She walked in the first day, started taking attendance, and Lincoln Spotted Eagle, sprawled out in his desk in the front row, drawled, "Hey! Misheéwea! We heard they saw you down in New Town, drunk and stoned, and dancing in the street!" Looking at the attendance log she asked, "Are you Lincoln?" "Yes, ma'am." "Well, Lincoln... I have not been downtown yet. I stopped drinking alcoholic beverages in 1972, and somehow I got through high school and college in the 1960s without ever using a recreational drug. However, the dancing in the street part...that could have been me!" The whole class burst out laughing.

She became a friend and mentor, helping many of them through tough times the next few years. What she said that changed Rod's life was, "If you indigenous people want to get back at the dominant society for what they did to your people, for the terrible injustices that still are being perpetrated, the best way to do that is to stop drinking. That's how you are being exterminated legally." He thought about that every time he heard of an alcohol-related death or accident. He got drunk once, puked his guts out and never drank again. Thanks, Mrs. H., wherever you are.

When he got to Marie Harper's apartment Rod let himself in, wearing gloves just in case it turned into a crime scene. He found no evidence of a baby living here — no bed, clothes, toys, nothing. On a hunch he checked the fridge and found bottles of formula and jars of baby food in the cupboard. He grabbed some of the formula to take to the hospital. Then he checked the laundry and pulled out two pieces of dirty baby clothes from the hamper, for forensics to check. *What the hell,* he thought. *This makes no sense at all. Baby clothes in the hamper, food in the fridge, but nothing else.*

In her desk, he found Marie's personal papers, which included her birth certificate but none for the baby. He found an obituary notice for Marie's mother, who had passed away a few months before. There were no other relatives named in the obituary, and it said that her husband, Marie's father, was deceased. Dead end in the worst sense. At this point there was no evidence of any wrongdoing, but his senses told him to expect something.

Heading back into town, as he passed the Ocean Spray cranberry warehouse his phone rang. It was the hospital. "Sergeant Kills On Top here," he answered.

"Sergeant, we need you to come to the hospital social worker's office as soon as you get back here. We did check Marie Harper's blood, and she could be the baby's mother!"

"I'm not surprised. What's happening with Jessica Wilson? Is her husband, Jimmy, there yet?"

"Yes, he got here about an hour ago. He's in the waiting room. We've told him nothing, except that his wife is in surgery and the baby is fine."

"OK. Let's keep it that way. I'll see you in a few minutes."

As he drove over the bridge into Aberdeen, it was beginning to get light, and he looked out over the log rafts floating in the river. This used to be a booming logging area, but the industry was hit hard in the '70s when the spotted owl, a threatened species, was found to be nesting throughout the forested coast. One little bird toppled a thriving community. It never recovered.

He puzzled now over this situation. What would ever possess a man to steal a dead woman's baby and pretend it was his? Maybe he panicked when he realized Marie was dead and didn't know what to do, so he took the baby to keep it safe? He went home to get the baby's things, he said, but he wouldn't have baby stuff if he had no baby. All the baby things were missing from Marie's house! That would explain it…did he know her?

At the hospital he met with the social worker and Dr. Ford. "It's good to meet you, Ms. Nolan. What have you found so far?" he asked.

"We looked up Jessica Wilson's medical records and she had a hysterectomy several years ago. The sock you gave us matches the one the baby had on. As Dr. Ford told you, we believe Marie Harper is the baby's mother. What do we do now?"

"Keep the baby safe and I'll go talk with Jimmy," answered Rod. "Thanks for your diligence and I'll be back as soon as I know where we're at."

As he waited for the elevator, Rod reached in his pocket and touched the medicine pouch his grandfather had given him when he gave Rod his spirit name, Walks with Bears. In the pouch was a piece of bear root, and a small rock shaped like a sitting bear. He worried it around in his pocket, thinking about the sign that the I.T. Director at Mandaree High School used to have hanging on his wall: "Ah, The World Is Such A Wonderful Place, If It Weren't For The People In It!" *That about sums it up, sometimes,* thought Rod. *What to do now?*

He grabbed two coffees from the vending machine, strolled into the waiting room, and sat next to Jimmy, offering him a coffee. "I got it with cream and sugar. Wasn't sure what you took."

"Thanks. That's perfect." Jimmy took the cup.

"So, they say your little girl's going to be fine. She's sure a cutie. How old is she?"

"Six months. She was born October 14th."

"What's her name?"

"Heather. Heather Lily Wilson." He smiled at the detective, nervously.

"Are you sure that isn't Heather Lily Harper?" Rod watched his reaction, saw him tense.

"What are you talking about? That's our baby, Jessie's and mine."

"Well, the thing is, Jimmy, Heather doesn't have a blood type that could have come from Jessica. And, we know that Jessica had a hysterectomy. But the baby could be Marie Harper's, the woman you hit. A DNA test will prove it. I found a sock in Marie's car that matches the one Heather had on when she was admitted. What I don't understand is why you would do such a foolish thing. Why would you take her baby?"

Jimmy looked up at Rod, then back down at his hands, trying to figure out how much to tell him without implicating himself in anything criminal. "She's my baby too. Check my DNA. It will prove it." He looked at Rod again, smiling.

"What the hell are you telling me, that you killed your baby's mother and then stole the child from her?"

"No, not on purpose! Marie and I had a one-night thing a year ago this past January. I didn't know she got pregnant. Tonight, when I went over to that car, I saw it was Marie, and that she was dead. I saw the baby. I just took her. I didn't want her to be in the car with her dead mama."

Rod watched him, waiting to see if more would come. Nothing. "OK...I get that. But there's this other thing. I went out to Marie's apartment to find information about next-of-kin. There was nothing there to indicate she had a baby except for formula and baby food, and dirty clothes in the hamper. Everything else was gone. I didn't find a birth certificate either. I'm wondering if I go out to your place if I will find the baby's things. You said you didn't know Marie had a baby, yet you knew her name and birthdate. Will I find her birth certificate at your place, Jimmy?"

For a moment Rod thought Jimmy was going to react violently, as he stiffened in his chair, turned, and gave Rod a hostile look. Just as quickly he leaned over, elbows on his knees, hands covering his face. Finally, he sat up, crossed his arms and said, "I took the spare house key and insurance card from Marie's purse and went to her place. I found Heather's birth certificate and figured she had to be mine, because of the timing. She looks like me too! I took all of the baby stuff and took it to our house. I didn't think beyond that. I got married a few months ago. Jessie can't have kids, as you know. I'm sorry Marie's dead, but if this is my kid, I want to raise her with Jessie!"

Rod leaned back against the couch, took a sip of his coffee, and stared at this man with his unbelievable story. "Crap, Jimmy...you sure got your ass in a sling. I've never heard of anything like this before. I should arrest you for burglary. I'm going to have to call my Chief about this. The hospital can keep Heather here for a few days under observation. Now, let's go see about your wife."

CHAPTER SIX

When they got to the surgical floor, Dr. Ford was consulting with the neurologist, Dr. Singh. They introduced themselves and Dr. Singh explained what had transpired so far.

They had done an MRI on Jessica to see how extensive the damage was to her throat. The twig from the tree had entered the left side of her neck, but had not severed the artery. They were able to operate and found that the vagus nerve, which branches out from the brain along the left and right vocal cords, and innervates the larynx, had been nicked by the twig, causing some damage. She would not be able to speak for a week or so, but her vocal cord would recover and she would talk again. However, the MRI also showed another issue. Dr. Singh asked Jimmy if Jessica had suffered from headaches.

"Yeah, crazy ones! There wasn't anything she could take to make them stop. Sometimes they started up from just a sneeze, or if she bent over for a while. It was nuts!"

"Well, we found a congenital condition called Chiari Malformation that causes those headaches, and other issues too, we believe. Part of her brain is pushing down into the spinal cord, pressing on the nerves. She's been living with this since birth. Sometimes it doesn't cause too many problems, but this accident seems to have jarred it further. She is having difficulty breathing now with throat closures from that, compounded by the operation we just performed to remove the stick."

Jimmy looked at Rod, helplessly. "Let's see if we are clear on this," the detective said. "Part of Jessica's brain is shoved into her spinal cord. The accident made it worse and she is having difficulty breathing because of it?"

"Basically, yes," answered Dr. Singh. She should have surgery for it immediately. What that entails is removing a small piece of her skull at the back of the brain, and slitting the lamina that covers the spine over the top three vertebrae. These two procedures will provide enough room for the cerebellar tonsils to pull back up enough to take the pressure off her spinal cord. If she doesn't have the surgery, the breathing issue may worsen and she could suffocate. We need your consent, Mr. Wilson, and I can start the procedure. She is still in the recovery room, under sedation from the other surgery. If she has this surgery those headaches will be relieved, I believe, and the breathing issue will dissipate."

"Go on ahead, then. I know she will be happy to get rid of those headaches. Can I see her before?"

"Yes, the nurse will take you back for a minute."

Rod walked next to Jimmy, amazed that the guy was holding up under the pressure of the accident, his wife's condition, and the discovery of the baby girl. "I'm going to have to stay with you under the circumstances. I hope you understand," he said, apologetically.

"No problem, man. I appreciate the company, and the translation with the doctor. I still don't know what he said, but if Jessie needs it, I'll sign for it."

Jessica's throat was bandaged, and a laceration on her forehead had been stitched, as well. Her right cheek was rubbed raw where the branch had scraped her, barely missing her eye.

Rod stood there watching Jimmy watch Jessica; saw his visceral reaction to the damage his wife had endured. He put his hand on Jimmy's arm. "You know they say something good comes out of every bad thing. Maybe the good in this is that she will get the operation that helps her out of the pain she has been in. And maybe you'll get to raise your beautiful baby girl."

The nurse came in with the papers for Jimmy to sign. "You might as well go home and get some sleep," she said. "The doctor has scheduled her surgery for 9:00 a.m. so you won't be able to see her before noon."

Jimmy sat down in a chair by the bed and read over the papers. "This has a lot of bad things in here, Sergeant. It even says she could die. I don't want to sign this giving them the right to do something that could kill her." He looked at Jessica, tears welling in his eyes.

"They have to say that, Jimmy, so you know that there is the possibility, and it covers their butt if it goes sideways. The other option is to not sign, wait until she wakes up, and they tell her everything. Then she can decide if she wants the operation."

"Yeah, maybe I should do that. I don't want her to wake up and be mad at me 'cause I let them cut out part of her skull! She's already got to deal with the fact that I have a baby."

Geez, Rod thought, *the baby should be the least of his worries.* He said, "The doctor did mention that throat closing stuff. That would worry me. What if you don't sign the papers, they don't operate, and she has one of those episodes and suffocates. Would you rather live with her dying, or maybe being mad at you? She survived that wreck. It would be a shame to have her die now, of something that can be fixed."

"Shit, I didn't think of that. This is hard." He sat shaking his head, tears running down his cheeks. "I thought she died in the wreck. Her

25

pulse stopped and I thought she was dead. When the paramedics revived her, I felt like the luckiest man alive. I got another chance with my new bride. You are right. I don't want to take a chance on her dying from that breathing thing 'cause I'm scared of her reaction. The right thing to do is sign this so they can help her." He wiped his eyes with his sleeve, signed the papers, got up and took them out to the nurse's station.

Rod walked out with Jimmy, said "See ya later," got in his car, and headed for the Aberdeen police station to shower, get a nap, and check on the legality of Jimmy and Jessica keeping Heather.

After a good sleep, a shower, and a few phone calls, Rod had enough information to feel confident in his next step.

CHAPTER SEVEN

Jimmy was in the waiting room when Rod arrived at the hospital around 11:00 a.m.

"Hey! Here's the deal. We'll ask for a paternity test today. If it proves you are Heather's father, then we petition Child Protective Service for you to take her, and have Jessica named as her adoptive mother. There shouldn't be any problem, since I can't find a next-of-kin for Marie. Regarding your entry to Marie's apartment and taking the stuff, my Chief is waiting on pressing charges on that, to see if you are Heather's father."

"Oh, I'm sure I'm her father," he said, smiling.

"Huh. Convenient for you, innit? Of all the cars that could have been in that intersection at that moment, it just happened to be you. That doesn't seem like a coincidence. I had a teacher once who would have called that a 'God Wink'...synchronicity...something like that."

"Yeah. I couldn't believe it myself when I looked in and saw Marie there. And when I saw the baby, I just knew it was mine! Jessie is going to be so happy — at least I hope so. I mean, she wouldn't be mad, would she? I was with Marie a long time ago, before I met Jessie. I had no idea she had a baby from that night."

"What, you never saw her again?"

"Nah...I didn't have her phone number, and a couple of weeks later, when I went back to her house, she had moved."

Dr. Singh walked in just then, taking off his cap and wiping his face with it. "Everything went well, gentlemen. I'm glad we did that surgery. There was so little room for the cerebellar tonsils to pull back into the skull that I couldn't replace the piece of skull I removed. I would normally put in a piece of pigskin. I had to put her scalp back over her brain with nothing in between. She's got to be careful not to fall. If anything penetrates her scalp it could go right into her brain! She's in recovery, and you will be able to see her in about an hour. I'll come and get you when we wake her. I want you to hear everything we tell her, so you understand, and can reassure her, and tell her the news about the baby. Meanwhile, I heard you are to take a DNA test to prove paternity. Why don't you go to the nurses' station to get that arranged while you wait." Jimmy left, and as the doctor walked out of the room he turned and said to Rod, "Sergeant, this goes to the top of my Unbelievably Strange list!" By the time Jimmy had completed his paperwork and given the swab for the DNA they were summoned to the recovery room.

Jessica was lying on her side, the back of her head bandaged now, in addition to the dressings on her wounds. The doctor finished checking her and gently turned her, adjusting a pillow behind her shoulders.

"Jessica, wake up," he said, hovering over her. "Jessica? Wake up, now. Jimmy is here."

They watched her as she slowly roused out of the leftover anesthetic fog, looked around, tried to focus her eyes, then closed them. "Jessica, you need to wake up now. I'm Dr. Singh. You are in the hospital. Let me tell you why."

Why is he calling me Jessica? She opened her eyes again, and looked around the room, stopping on Jimmy. *What is he doing here?*

Rod, watching her intently, thought, *That's fear on her face. I wonder if he abuses her?*

"Jessica, I'm Dr. Singh. Please blink if you understand what I'm telling you." She blinked at him. "Good. You were in an automobile accident last night. Your throat was badly injured. I've repaired it but you won't be able to speak for a couple of weeks. I'm going to explain some things to you, and I've brought a whiteboard for you to write on as you have questions. OK?"

Thirsty. So thirsty. She reached for the marker, and he held the whiteboard for her as she wrote, shakily, WATER.

"I'm sorry. You are on an IV drip for a while and will not be able to swallow. But I'll rub an ice chip over your lips for you. Jimmy, you'll be able to do this for her." Jimmy stepped up to the bed to see how the doctor did it, and she shrank back, closing her eyes.

I was in an accident. Holy Mother, I remember. I died! Heather! James took Heather. I prayed to God I could be her mom again, but in the other woman's body. That must be Jessica. I'm Jessica now. James is her husband! She reached for the marker again, and wrote, HEATHER.

The three men looked at each other. *Well, here's a new wrinkle,* thought Rod.

"Did you doctors talk about the baby in front of her?" demanded Jimmy.

"No," Dr. Singh responded. "I don't think the nurses would either."

"Well, how in hell did she find out?"

Oh damn. I'm not supposed to know about her. I DREAMED OF HEATHER she wrote.

"Jessica, we'll get to that in a minute. For now, Heather is fine, and waiting to meet you. I need to tell you about what we discovered about your headaches, and what treatment we did." She nodded for him to continue. "We did an MRI to learn how much damage was done to

29

your throat in the accident. We discovered a birth anomaly that has caused your headaches and other symptoms throughout your life. I will go into more detail when you've recovered from the operation and rested more. The problem was compounded in the wreck and threatened your life, so we had to do a surgery. We removed a small piece of your skull in the back. Your headaches should be much better, and hopefully gone. Any questions?"

She wrote MIRROR.

While the doctor called for a mirror, he suggested Jimmy tell her about Heather. Jimmy sat on the edge of the bed. She watched him, warily. "Jessie, the accident was bad, really bad. The lady in the other car didn't make it. She had her baby girl with her. I recognized the lady, Jessie. I had dated her early last year. Her name was Marie. I didn't know she got pregnant."

Her eyes narrowed as the impact of his story hit her.

"Jessie, the baby is Heather. I took a DNA test to prove she is mine. We get to raise her, Jessie. I promised you we would adopt, but this is better. This is my baby and you will be her mom."

You dirty rat bastard. You raped me, left me, killed me, and now get my baby??? She closed her eyes, and began to breathe slowly, deep breaths, in and out as she relaxed and thought it through. *Choice. I made a choice and I asked for this chance to raise Heather. I remember my life and know nothing about Jessica's. How is this going to work? How am I going to pick up the pieces of a life I know nothing about? How can I live with this man? Oh, my God, what have I done to myself? I asked for a chance to raise Heather. I gave her a chance to have me in her life. I have to protect myself, while I figure this out. I can't talk, that will help some. Time. I need time.* Finally, a plan in her mind, she picked up the marker and wrote, WHO ARE YOU

Again, the three men looked at each other, in shock. *Well, hells bells, this just gets better and better!* thought Rod.

"You must have amnesia, Jessica, brought on by the accident, and possibly exacerbated by the surgeries," said Dr. Singh. "It's not uncommon. Do you remember anything at all?" She shook her head.

"Well, you will be recovering here in the hospital for at least a week. Jimmy, it would be good for you to tell her the stories of her life that you know. That may help her remember. It will come back, I promise. This kind of amnesia is only temporary."

No doc, I don't think so. I don't think I'll be remembering a life I never lived. She took the mirror he handed her and gazed into hazel green eyes in a face full of freckles, bruises, scrapes, bandages, and curly amber hair poking out wherever it could. *So, this is the new me. Not bad. Not bad at all.*

"Would you like to see Heather now?" asked the doctor.

Oh, yes! But no. I don't want her to see me like this the first time. She picked up the marker. FACE IS SCARY WAIT IS SHE BEING LOVED

"Yes, she is loved and held by everyone here. We call her our miracle child... a miracle that she survived that wreck unharmed, and that she has her father and you, now. She is young enough that she will adjust quickly to her new family."

Exhausted, Jessica closed her eyes, and the three men watched as tears slipped from the corners, and made their way down her battered face.

CHAPTER EIGHT

Rod decided to go home, to the reservation, and check in at his own police station in the morning, where he would file the report about the fatality. As he drove through the forest roads along the ocean he rolled the window down, inhaling the briny air, stopping once to watch a small black bear cross the road. "Aho, brother!" he chuckled. He mused about the connection between the people and the animals. The Natives out here, all along the coast, were tied to the sea and its creatures. Whaling and salmon fishing go back generations. The ceremonies each year to thank the earth mother for the bountiful harvest reminded him of the sacred ceremonies back home, centered around the buffalo.

He pulled into his sister's place, got out, and stretched, marveling at the giant cedar trees edging the woods behind the house. He remembered Mrs. H. reading that book to them in class, *SNOW FALLING ON CEDARS,* and not being able to imagine trees that size. Now he lived with these trees, friends, like she described.

He walked among them, their fresh green boughs sweeping gently over the top of the sweat lodge he had built behind the house. He needed a sweat tonight. Walking the worn path through the grass, he was grateful for Samantha. Older than him by three years, his sister had known she wanted to be a doctor since she was small, and went with their grandmother to the clinic every week for her dialysis treatment. Sam had studied hard in school, then in college, finally ending up with a full scholarship to the University of Washington medical school. Her determination to create a good life for herself had made it easier for him. She had bought this little piece of land when she got the job here, and had a house built by the tribal construction crew. He climbed the steps to the back porch, sat on the rocking chair, and kicked off his boots. Pulling off his police department ball cap, he hung it on a hook beside the door and went into the kitchen. The sunny yellow paint was in direct defiance of his black mood.

Sam was sitting at the table, still in her scrubs. Her long, black hair was piled on top of her head, held by a scrunchie. Her eye glasses, which she only needed for reading and other close work, perched on top of her head. Occasionally she had a Tootsie Roll pop, a pencil, a thermometer, or some other tool poked in her hair, as well. Rod had always thought of her as a little crow, her hair a nest full of useful items to be traded when necessary. "Hey...long time no see — you working a case? I made some stew and fry bread. Sit down and eat with me." He took off his holster, removed the clip from his pistol and hung it all on the coat rack. He washed up at the kitchen sink, dished up some supper, and joined her. He told her about the accident, and what had happened since.

"Geez, bro, that's nasty, innit? I knew that lady. She did our coding. She put her baby in our child care center whenever she needed to work in the office. It was the only white baby. I remember walking by the preschool room one day and there sits Marie, reading a book to the kids. She was a great reader. The kids were hanging on her words. Behind her was the window, and all of a sudden there was a young man standing outside, the sun shining on him, making him glow. He had on a buckskin shirt, and feathers in his hair. Marie saw the kids all look up, over her head, out the window. She turned and looked, saw the young man, then asked the kids, 'Who is that?' 'It's an Indian!' they whooped. 'Well, you are Indians,' she answered. 'Yeah, but he's a real Indian!' one of the boys yelled out. It made me laugh and sad at the same time. We have been so marginalized over time even our own people have no idea who we are."

"That's the plight of all cultures outside the dominant one," Rod said, taking a big bite of fry bread. "History was written by the subjugators. They had to make us 'less than' in order to sell their stories to their people. Unfortunately, the books and movies portrayed us as the warriors who had to be eradicated, but things are changing. People think for themselves now, investigate, and learn the truth."

"Hey, speaking of the truth, mom called yesterday and told me that the tribal historian from Fort Berthold, and some other elders are writing a book about the true story of Sacagawea, how she actually was Hidatsa/Crow, not Shoshone. It's called, *SACAGAWEA: THEY GOT IT WRONG*. Her relatives have proven, with DNA, her genetic background, I think. Anyway, it's going to be a good read!"

They finished their meal. "Did you happen to put some food out for the grandfathers? I want to have a sweat tonight, before I go back to town tomorrow."

"Sure did," she replied. "I'll join you. I'll call P.J. to come over and get the rocks ready."

A few minutes later she came outside, wearing a sweat dress their mom had made for her, years ago. She grabbed a hose and filled the bucket of water to use in the lodge, carefully placing it on the ground next to the structure. She took a plastic ladle from her hair and put it in the water. The lodge had been a part of their culture for centuries, as sacred a place to them as a church or synagogue was to others. A

35

dome-shaped structure, some compare to the shape of an igloo, the lodge varies in size. Between five and six feet in height, it was formed with red willow saplings, crossing over each other, forming the dome. The saplings were then covered with blankets and tarps, creating a dark, womb-like structure. The entry faces west, with a flap to bring down as in closing a door, once the people are inside. Their lodge could seat eight people comfortably, on the ground. Sam had heard someone once say this was the Indian's "sauna," which kind of raised her hackles. Yes, it provided physical benefits as participants took part in the cleansing ritual. But it was primarily a spiritual experience, an opportunity to be in the safety of the lodge, with family and friends, to pray to the Creator of all.

After Rod had cleaned up the kitchen, he went into his room, opened his cedar chest, and took out some tobacco and a piece of red cloth. He carefully placed a handful of tobacco in the center of the cloth, folded it, tied it off, and placed it in a small basket. He opened a large Ziploc bag which contained dried cedar that had hung in the garage over the winter. He had stripped it from the boughs when it was bone dry, rubbing the needles between his fingers until they crumbled into tiny pieces, until he had a pile of aromatic cedar sprigs. He scooped a handful out of the bag into the basket and picked it up. Grabbing his hand drum, he went out to the lodge, and noted the plate of food sitting on top, an offering to the spirits.

P.J. had built a blazing fire, and in the middle of it were red hot rocks, ready to be brought into the lodge. Rod handed him some tobacco, as thanks. Two other neighbors were standing there, in their shorts, ready to go in. Rod grabbed his hand drum and the basket, nodded to the four directions, then got down and crawled into the lodge. He circled around the hole in the ground, which had been dug in the center. He continued on all fours, until he was next to the entrance, where he sat. He hung the red tobacco tie over one of the willow branches that supported the lodge. Sam passed the bucket in, then crawled in and sat next to him. The other two took their places. P.J.'s job was to take care of the fire and the rocks, praying as he did so. He placed a pitchfork loaded with seven rocks, scalding hot from the fire, into the pit in the ground, then pulled the flap down over the opening, leaving the other four in blackness, a glow from the red rocks the only light. Rod sprinkled a handful of cedar over the rocks, and they spit twinkles into the air, the aroma comforting the four of them as they began this ancient ritual bath of the spirit. Next, he poured a ladle full of water over the rocks, and they sizzled thanks as the hot vapors rose and surrounded the humans who would sing to them. Rod hit the drum, and began the four directions song, inviting the ancestors to join them.

Sam noticed, with a grateful heart, the small blue lights as they entered, hovering over them, at the top of the lodge.

As they went through the four rounds, more water being poured, the air became heavy and hot. They sang songs in Hidatsa, Lakota, and the local language of the people here, lower Chehalis. Only a few of the elders spoke the original language anymore. They were teaching the youth, so it didn't die out.

During the prayer round, they prayed for healing for the people, gave their personal prayers, and finally gave thanks, hiyu maśi, to the Creator for the lives they had been given. After each round, Rod passed a ladle of water for them to drink, and P.J. opened the flap, so they could go out, stretch, and drink in the night air, before the next round. Afterward they sat on benches outside, around the fire. Rod loaded the sacred pipe with pure tobacco, and they smoked it; the smoke carrying their prayers up to the heavens.

CHAPTER NINE

In the morning, Rod made breakfast for Samantha before she left for work. As they scarfed down sausage, eggs and waffles, he shared his conflicted feelings about Jessica with her. "Hey," he asked. "There's something that is bugging me about this woman, Jessica. When she woke up, she looked at her husband, Jimmy, like she was scared to death of him, yet later asked who he was. And she wrote Heather on the whiteboard as soon as she realized she had been in an accident. Yet no one had told her about the baby. She said she had dreamed of it. I know things come to people in dreams but this didn't seem real. It was as though she was caught out, and made it up. And then there is the husband. It's all too neat, him having a baby with a lady he had dated, and not knowing. Then he marries a woman who can't have kids and they want to adopt. Then he accidentally crashes into his baby's mom and kills her. Now he and his wife get the baby."

"Geez...do you think he crashed into her on purpose so they could raise the baby?"

"I'm wondering that, yeah...I'm wondering that." He looked at her and shook his head.

"Trust your gut, brother." Sam reached for another piece of toast. "You're right...if she has amnesia, how would she remember to be afraid of him? Doesn't make sense, huh? Now the baby thing...I don't know. If you think there's something wrong you need to stay close to her, somehow. Spend some time with her. Get her to trust you. Do you trust her? Maybe she might know something, or not know she knows something, hey, that could help you figure it all out. Otherwise 'n that, I don't know what to tell you."

Rod took his time driving back up the highway toward Westport, thinking about the question Sam had asked him, did he trust Jessica? His grandmother had taught him about trust when he was small by giving him a jar with a hundred pennies in it. She said that was her trust for him — 100%. Whenever he did something untrustworthy, she took away a penny, putting it in another jar. He quickly learned how to get the pennies back and keep the jar full. He did that with the people in his life now too, keeping a running tally in his mind. So far, Jessica had a full jar. If he got to the point where he believed Jimmy might have killed Marie on purpose, he would need to question her. He would have to trust that she would put the baby and herself first.

Deciding to take a walk on the beach before heading back inland, he turned left on Ocean Avenue, passed the old lighthouse and parked in the lot for the state park. He walked quickly up the sidewalk, feeling the change in his gait when he stepped onto the dunes. How he loved these dunes. The scrubby pines and long feathery grasses reminded him of walks on the prairies near Mandaree, on his reservation in North Dakota.

As he passed the condos that had been built on the dunes, he shook his head. People with money, he thought. They always want to have the best land closest to the water.

Only this time it backfired. That lighthouse way back down the road had once stood on the edge of the land here, right on the ocean, a beacon for ships passing. Over the decades the ocean had shifted, due partly to berms that had been built to keep the water from destroying the town, and partly to Mother Nature and the effects of the moon on the tides. Whatever the reason, the ocean had pulled back, the dunes had reached far out into the sea, and the people had bought them up and built on them.

Over the past few years, king tide storms in winter had battered the shore, each year taking back a little more. Several hundred yards of landscaped beauty in front of the condos had been shortened to a twenty-foot piece of grass between the buildings and the beach; and then their nemesis, the water, encroached on them. Hoping to keep the dunes from eroding further, the condo association had built a wall of sand, twenty feet high, a testament to man's stupidity. He looked at the wall that had been constructed; sand packed in with coconut grass. In front of it cobbled stone was banked against it, put there to slow the impact of the waves when they battered the shore. Over the past year, the sea had brought and dropped tons of driftwood, heaping it up against the cobbled stone, like a pile of Lincoln logs waiting for children to come along and build a fort. It stretched from the edge of the park, all along the front of the condos, twenty feet high. How long would it take for that to erode, he wondered, how many storms? Why do people keep doing the same crazy things over and over, without learning?

All they had to do was drive down to the reservation, near Tokeland, and see the historic Washaway Beach, where a whole town now lay underwater; a town built in the late 1800's, and flooded during the mid-20th century. The ocean gradually took it, street by street, until all that is left is the occasional remembrance that floats up onto the sand, thrown up by the sea that had swallowed it.

Rod stepped down onto the beach and turned south, bracing himself as he walked into the bitter April wind, glad it would be at his back when he turned around later. Knowing he would have a bit of reprieve from the biting, blasting gusts when he retraced his steps made it easier to lean into it now.

He passed several man-made structures created from driftwood, gifts from the sea. His favorite was a small collection of log constructions on the beach; small castles created near a cross that had been built up on the dunes. He had seen children climbing on them. He had talked to a woman down there once as he petted her dogs, a yellow lab and a black poodle. She called the structures Christ's Village, because of the cross.

She pointed out to him the two tall platforms people had built for the eagles. They had stood and watched as a bald eagle landed gracefully, the carcass of a dead fish in its talons. It sat ripping bites off, gobbling them down, glaring stink-eye at an eagle that had landed on the other end of the platform, waiting, hopefully, for a taste.

Today, as he approached Christ's Village, he saw those same dogs lying in the sand, and that woman standing at the bottom of one of the structures, looking up, and laughing. At the top of a driftwood tower was an old desk chair someone had managed to haul up there. The chair was tied with pieces of rope salvaged from crab pots that had washed up on the beach. Precariously leaning now, and listing, like a crab float bobbing in an ocean swell, the chair held a second woman. Her long, white hair blew around her head, cloud-like. How in the heck had she climbed up there, he wondered. How would she get down? Apparently, they were discussing that very problem when Rod walked up and offered to help. He held the makeshift driftwood ladder as she made her way creakily down, grabbing her friend's hand as she neared the bottom. "Woohoo," she yelled, as she jumped the last three feet. "That's something I can cross off my bucket list!" Rod stepped back, scratched his head in amazement, and said, "Mrs. H?"

She stood there, gaping, hands on hips, then flew through the air, her arms wrapping around his waist as she squeezed the breath out of him. "Rodney Kills On Top! Am I seeing things? I just asked the Great Spirit to help me get down from there, but never did I think He would send an angel boy from the North Dakota badlands!"

"Mrs. H. What are you doing here???" He returned her hug, shaking his head.

"Did you forget I'm from Washington? The better question is, what are YOU doing here? Judy, this is Rod, a student of mine from North Dakota. Rod, Judy and I taught in the same school the past eleven years, before we retired." They nodded, and Judy told her they had met before, she and Rod, at this very spot. "And Rod, just so you know...I'm not Mrs. H. anymore. He flew the coop years ago. You call me Becky. Becky Farmer. I took my own last name back."

"Well, Mrs. H...uh, Becky, I have a lot to tell you and the wind's picking up. Can we head back and I'll fill you in?" As they walked up the beach, he shared his story with her. Judy invited him to come back to the condo with them for lunch.

CHAPTER TEN

"What an achievement, Rod!" exclaimed Becky, using his arm for support as they climbed back up the dunes. I am so happy Samantha is out here too. I can't wait to see her. And a doctor! And you are a detective. I'm not surprised, you were both such good students. Your mom must be so proud."

"Yes, she is that. She was here last summer for a visit. We want her to move out here, but there are so many aunties that need her there, so she stays."

Judy washed the dog's feet with a hose she kept on the patio, and they all left their sandy shoes at the door as they entered the condo. While Judy got lunch ready, Rod walked around looking at the photos on the walls. "Becky took all of those," Judy said. "She helped me decorate too. She made this place into a beach paradise!"

"Do you stay here too?" Rod asked Becky.

"No, I have a little cabin down the road. I wanted some space around me for a garden. I come here when I want to be at the beach, and to see my friend."

"It was smart of you, Judy, to buy one of these way back from the beach. At least you won't fall in the ocean!" Rod laughed.

"Not in my lifetime, I hope! That's what I thought when I bought it!"

As Rod stood, looking at a series of photos she had shot of the eagles on the platforms, Becky watched him, tenderly. His hair, raven black, was tied back in a braid. He wore glasses now, which made him look serious, more mature. His long, lanky shape had transformed into solid muscle. He looked dependable. *What a wonderful man he grew into*, she thought.

She remembered the year his cousins had fallen through the ice, and drowned. How people thought he may have been with them. That next summer, he had been playing basketball on the court outside the school, and she had invited him to come in for a lemonade, to get out of the sun's blast. They had sat at the kitchen table, his brown hands wrapped around the sweating glass. Tipping it a bit, watching the ice float through the lemonade, he blurted, "I want to tell you something..."

"Sure. Anything. Go ahead." She waited, intuitively knowing he was about to reveal the truth about that awful, wintery dusk when the boys had drowned.

He sat, for a bit, looking at that ice floating. She waited. He finally drank it down, got up and left, without a word.

Now, here, thirteen years later, she put her hand on his arm. He looked at her. "If I had a son, you would be him. I am so happy you are in my life again."

Judy called them to lunch. As Rod dug into a salad loaded with crab fresh off a boat that morning, he looked at the mobile hanging in the dining room window. It was a chunk of driftwood, shaped like a fish. There was a piece of blue beach glass in a small hole where the eye would be, and wire lines hanging down, like pieces of kelp; the wires, wrapped around agates, shells, and rocks, swayed in the breeze coming in the window. "Did you do that, Judy?" he asked.

"No, that's another one of Becky's creations," she answered. "She has a lot of talent!"

"She had creative talent as a teacher too. One year they turned the Christmas pageant at the school over to her, the whole shebang, grades K-12. She had our drama class rewrite the nativity scene as though it happened on the reservation with our people. The three kings were chiefs from other tribes. While we acted it out, each grade sang a song that fit into the play. It was great. The families loved it.

Your people are lucky that your religious history was written down. We kept ours alive orally. White Buffalo Calf Woman, for instance. She was a messenger from the Creator too, we believe, for our people. But when it's written down, in a book, it seems to carry more weight."

"You are right, Rod. If the world knew more about indigenous peoples' beliefs and ways, I think this planet would be in better shape!" Judy replied.

"Yeah, and it would be a happier place, too, that's for sure," chimed Becky. "I laughed more the years I lived with your people than in the whole rest of my life, I think!"

"You sure made the whole town laugh with that last song you wrote with the middle schoolers. I will never forget that!" Rod chuckled.

"I did not write that. That was strictly their song!" she countered.

"Tell me," Judy urged. "I never heard this one."

Becky sat back, smiling as she remembered. "Every grade was prepared with their part of the pageant, except the sixth through eighth graders. They refused. No one could get them to take part. Finally, the week before, we had a school meeting with them and their teachers. I got hard on them, told them their parents would be there. They would get to see all the brothers and sisters perform, and then I would have to get up and tell them, 'Sorry, folks, no middle school performance. Your kids said no.' They discussed it and finally agreed to do a song if it could be about reservation life. So, we rewrote the 'Twelve Days of Christmas' using things in their everyday life. It started out with a prairie chicken in an oak tree. That wasn't too bad. It had mangy dogs, knocked-up cats, and it went so downhill from there. I figured I'd lose my job, for sure. The art teacher worked with them to illustrate the whole thing. We saved it for last and I got up and said something like, 'You know your kids at this age. Please accept this song in the spirit they intend it. They wrote it with love and laughter.' By the time they got to the sixth verse the audience was singing along, 'Five junker cars...four mangy dogs, three knocked-up cats, two bingo cards, and a prairie chicken in an oak tree.' They loved it."

"Yeah, and you were awarded teacher of the year. We never forgot you, Becky."

"I never got over you all either. It was the best of times. There was never a day that I didn't laugh about something."

"Yeah, well, laughter is sometimes the only thing that gets us through a situation. Speaking of which, Judy, did you ever hear what Custer's last words were? He was standing on top of a hill at Little BigHorn, watching a shitload of warriors charge up and he knew it was the end. He turned to his aide, and said, 'Well, it's better than going back to North Dakota.'"

They all laughed as they finished their lunch. "Becky, you always said, 'There is a reason for everything.' I believe that. I believe there is a reason we met up today. Will you help me figure something out on a case I'm working on?" asked Rod.

"Of course. I have all the time in the world," she answered.

"I don't have much time, though," he said. "I have to get back to Aberdeen. I might need your help with this woman. Didn't you tell us that you had some degree in speech therapy?"

"I got my minor in speech pathology when I was studying to be a teacher, yes. But I never did practice it, except in the regular classroom a bit with students who needed help. Why?"

"Well, there is this woman in the hospital who was in a car wreck. A tree pierced her throat and they had to operate. It nicked something and she can't talk. The doctor said, with therapy, she will be able to talk again. She has temporary amnesia too. I have a feeling this crash may not have been an accident. I was thinking maybe I could introduce you, and you could help her while she is in the hospital. It's critical that we find out if she knows anything as she gets her memory back. Could you come in someday this week and meet her? By then I'll know more about what we need."

"Absolutely. Put my number in your phone and call me when you need me." He took her number, hugged both her and Judy, said "See ya later," and left.

"What a hunk!" Judy exploded with laughter. "Too bad we're old enough to be his grandmas!"

CHAPTER ELEVEN

Jessica woke, her head throbbing so loudly she could hear her heartbeat. Keeping her eyes closed, she listened to the sounds of the hospital... ambulance outside, footsteps in the hall, a cart rolling past, muffled voices at the nurses' station. They had moved her from Critical Care to a private room early this morning after Dr. Singh's visit. He had gone over everything again, assuring her that her voice and memory would return.

She had just looked at him. Again, he had told Jimmy to tell her stories about their life together, and any he knew about her previous life.

Jimmy had taken her hand between his. She controlled her knee-jerk reaction, wanting to pull her hand away, yet fighting the temptation, knowing she needed to resist the hate as it welled up in her. He said, "Doctor, I will do my best. I can't wait to hear her sweet drawl again."

"She has a drawl?" Dr. Singh smiled.

"Hell, yeah! She grew up in Kentucky, and her voice just drips sorghum!"

"Sorghum...what is that?"

"It's sweet, kind of like molasses. They make it in Kentucky from sorghum grain."

What have I done to myself, she thought. *A drawl? I'm not drawling in my thoughts. My thoughts sound in my head just like my voice sounded before. When I talk will it come out in a drawl or will I have my own voice? What controls the sound that comes out...years of vibration of the vocal cords, or years of memory stored in the brain of how a voice should sound? If it comes out Marie's voice...can I blame the amnesia on forgetting how to drawl?...*and she drifted back into drug induced sleep.

Now awake again, head pounding, she opened her eyes to find Jimmy sitting, staring at her. His eyes had a soft shine she had not seen when she dated him that night. This was a different man entirely. Gentle and caring, he had hardly left her side.

She picked up the whiteboard. CAN I SEE HEATHER He picked it up, erased it, and wrote SURE LET ME GET THE BABY DOC She couldn't help it...she grinned, erased his, and wrote I CAN HEAR YOU DUMB SHIT I JUST CAN'T TALK Jimmy burst out laughing, "That's my Jessie!" He got up and left to ask a nurse to call the pediatrician.

I don't have her memories, but I must have her mouth. I have never called anyone a dumb shit in my life! Although I have a vague memory of calling him a rat bastard earlier. How does this work? Does her brain still retain the language it used before, that it's comfortable with?

Jimmy walked in with a pretty blonde in scrubs. "Hi! I'm Dr. Ford. I was here when they brought you in, and have been keeping up with Heather's pediatrician ever since. Jimmy said you waited to see Heather because of the injuries to your face. That was really thoughtful. The swelling has gone down even more since they removed the bandages. There is just a little discoloration around your eye and the dressing on the scalp wound. I think you look fine to be presented to your daughter! What do you think?"

Jessica nodded, eagerly. Dr. Ford went to the hallway, got the baby from a nurse, and slowly walked over to the bed, holding Heather in front of her, facing Jessica.

Oh God, Oh God! Thank you, dear Lord, for this second chance to love my sweet girl.

She waited quietly for Heather to notice her. The doctor sat, placing the baby between them. Jessica carefully reached out a finger and stroked her little arm. Heather looked up at her, then away. Jessica smiled, stroked her again, then ran her fingers up her arm like she used to. Heather giggled, pulled back, then held her arm out to play again. *This will work. We can do this. I will make you love me again, in time.*

"I have to get back to work," said Dr. Ford. "I would leave her with you, but I can't, because of hospital regulations, since the paternity isn't certain yet. But I will let the staff know that when anyone has time, they can bring her in to you for feeding and a visit."

Jessica nodded, in agreement.

As Dr. Ford left with Heather in her arms, Jessica began to shake with silent screams.

Jimmy, who had watched her with the baby, so natural, was shocked at her reaction. "Hey, Jessie, baby, don't cry." He tried to take her in his arms but she pushed him away, turning into the pillow, her grief growing by the second, until it seemed the entire room would explode with it. He ran to get help as she pounded the pillow and thrashed herself against the railed bed, letting that sound be the voice she couldn't cry out to let the world know what had happened. *Is this hell?* she screamed inside her head. *How am I going to do this? How can I? Please, God, you gave me this chance... tell me how to do this!*

Betty, the charge nurse, came in and gave her a sedative, explaining to Jimmy that it is not unusual to react after so much trauma. "Think about it...she's been in a terrible accident, had two major surgeries, lost her voice, her memory, and got a kid she didn't know her husband had, in the bargain. What's not to scream about?" She nudged him in the shoulder, grinning.

"Well, when you put it that way," he smiled back.

"Just be here for her. And go home to sleep. No more hanging out all night in that chair, or you will be a mess when she is ready to return to the world. Bring some of her things from home, pictures, that kind of stuff."

The next day when she woke, Jessica was surrounded by plants and photos. A beautiful quilt lay over her legs. She touched it, wondering.

"Your Grandma in Kentucky made that quilt for us when we got married. I called your folks, Jessie, and told them what happened. Your Mom wants to come out, but I asked her to wait until you're home, and she can help with the baby. They are really happy for us. Maybe you will have your memory back by then. I told them about the amnesia, that it is temporary, from the accident. Do you remember anything, yet?" he asked, hopefully.

Oh, yeah...I remember everything...every rotten thing about you, and I don't know what I can do about it. She shook her head no.

He spent the rest of the morning telling her what he knew about her early years, the stories she had told him.

"One of my favorite stories was when you tried to get rid of your freckles," he laughed. "Some of the boys in your class were teasing you about them. You went home and climbed the peach tree in the backyard, crying your eyes out. Your Granddaddy was working in the barn, and heard you. When you told him what had happened, he told you to come out to Red Lick Hollow to his place for the weekend. He said there would be a full moon, and he knew how to get rid of the freckles on a full moon. You did, and after supper your grandma put her canning kettle on the wood stove, filled it with water, and set it to boil. Your granddaddy gave you a gunny sack. He told you to go down into the gully at midnight and pick that sack full of morning glory flowers, bring them back, and put them in the kettle. When they had boiled for ten minutes, he said to strain the gunk out of the water, then put the water in the bathtub. You were supposed to soak in the water until it got cold and your freckles would disappear. You did exactly as he said. But when you put the colander in the sink and poured the concoction in you forgot to put a bowl underneath. All you had left was the gunk from the flowers. You soaked in that nasty stuff, but it didn't work. I'm glad...I love your freckles! And I love your voice, your drawl. I can't wait to hear you call me 'sugar,' again!"

As she lay there listening, she realized that this woman, Jessica, had been loved. She had two younger brothers and the tales Jimmy told her made her smile. She realized too, that whatever terrible things he had done, Jimmy loved Jessica. He was ecstatic about the baby. If she were going to make this work, she needed to begin building trust with this man, this Jimmy who wasn't the James she remembered.

They brought Heather in again, after lunch, and Jessica fed her. Then, while Jimmy held the baby, Jessica wrote SING THIS TO HEATHER — ONCE A WEE MOUSE HAD A WEE HOUSE AND IT WENT CREEPY CRAWLY ALL THE WAY HOME.

Jimmy snorted, "You gotta be kidding!"

She just sat there looking at him. He rolled his eyes and sang the verse. While he sang, Jessica ran her fingers up Heather's arm, ending up under her ear. The baby laughed and held her arm out to Jessica for more. *She's remembering this! She may not know me, but she remembers the things we did. Just wait, little one. I'll be talking in no time and you will grow to love me as your mama all over again.*

CHAPTER TWELVE

Day three. Rod was on his way back to Aberdeen when he got a call from the hospital again. This time they wanted him to go to the morgue to see the pathologist. *Now what?* he thought.

The pathologist met him at the door and escorted him to the autopsy room. He knew the body on the table must be Marie Harper.

"There is something you need to see, Sergeant Kills On Top." He pulled the sheet back, exposing Marie's face. It was bruised and her nose broken. Rod remembered the airbags in that model and year were faulty, and had been recalled. It wouldn't have made a difference, though. She had been torn practically in half when the car wrapped around the tree. As the sheet was pulled further down, the tops of her breasts came into his view, and he almost fell over, grabbing the table for support. On each breast, just above the nipple, was a circle scar, a burn, the exact size of a cigarette.

"From the way the skin has healed around those, I would say she received them about a year, to a year and a half ago," said the pathologist, looking directly at Rod. "Looks like your serial killer let one go. Either that or you have a very strange coincidence here."

Rod left the hospital, went to his car, and pulled some sage out of the glove box. He lit it carefully, moving the burning plant slowly around his head, down over his torso, and around his legs, cleansing himself from the vileness he had just seen, trying to wrap his mind around all that had transpired since yesterday. "Grandfather...see me, hear me, way down here, so far from you. Help me, please, to understand what you have shown me. Nux Baaga-aiza. All my relations."

Rod had worked with the Aberdeen police over the past four years on a serial rapist/killer case. Four bodies, all Aberdeen women, had been dropped on the Shoalwater Reservation, always in January. They had been branded on their breasts with a cigarette, a detail that had not been released to the news. The first one had been left next to a dumpster in a wooded area behind the casino. Double-bagged in large black lawn bags, the sanitation guy had thought it was leaves raked up from the golf course. Rod had been at the station when the call came in. It was his first dead body. He retched now, remembering the stench from body fluids and rotting flesh. The last killing was only three months ago. They had found her almost immediately, the black bags recognizable by now. Good thing, because the killer had choked this one viciously, breaking open her throat. If a bear had been near and smelled the blood, he would have ripped open that bag and spread that body all over the little cemetery where she had been dumped. If Marie were also a victim, that would have been January, 2017. That year they had not found anyone.

He sat in his car, thinking over the cases and the similarities. What are the possibilities? Marie was raped by the serial killer and got away, or the killer let her go, for some reason? She was also in a relationship with Jimmy around that time? Or Jimmy is the serial killer!

He drove to the police station, walked into the chief's office and closed the door. "We got ourselves a shit storm," he said.

Chief Dolan laughed at the term and offered him a cup of coffee. "What's up, Rod?

He filled her in on the accident and all that had happened since. When he got to the part about Marie's burns, she slammed her hand on the desk and hollered, "No friggin' way!"

"Yeah, way..." Rod retorted. "I can't believe it myself but there it is. There was no body that year. We all thought the killer had died or moved. Then the girl in January made us think he had been away, or in jail for a while on some other charge. Chief, there is a strong possibility that Jimmy Wilson is the killer. We need to get that paternity test done now, and make sure Jessie and the baby stay in the hospital while we look into this. If he is the killer, and that is his baby, maybe he knew it, and stalked Marie, and caused that wreck on purpose."

"You're right. I'll call the hospital and get the test expedited. I'll also call your police station and ask Chief Winters if you can continue to work this case with us. I want you and Carmen to go back through the evidence on all the cases and see if you can find anything linking them that we missed and see if Marie fits in somehow. There must be something connecting them that will lead us to Jimmy if it's him."

He went back to his cubicle, found Carmen reading through a file, and brought her up to speed. They decided she would pull Jimmy's work history for the past five years and comb through it to see if she could find anything they had missed. He would work backwards, look at Marie's life the past couple of years and see if it shed some light.

On the drive back out to Tokeland he thought about how, in his people's beliefs, everything is connected. There are reasons for everything. You take a person who does bad things, and usually you find something that was done to them, something horrific, that brought out the demon in them. *What are Jimmy's demons*, he wondered. He would check him out as soon as he finished at Marie's.

He let himself into Marie's with her keys, and settled down at her desk. He found the agency name on the rental agreement and called them. The agent who rented the house to Marie agreed to come over. While he waited, he went through her notebook he found in a drawer. She was meticulous, keeping her bank and credit card passwords in a list, on the back page. He pulled up each statement, downloaded it, and made a copy to go over later. He went back to January, 2017.

Then he found her work files. She worked as a medical coder, both for a clinic in Aberdeen, and for the tribe. He copied the details for those too, so he could stop by and let them know what had happened. Maybe someone there could fill in some pieces about her life.

The doorbell rang. He let the agent in, rain dripping from the bottom of her overcoat, as she removed it and hung it on the hall tree. "I will never get used to the rain here!" she exclaimed as they shook hands. "Where are you from?" he asked. "Arizona. I moved here last year to be closer to my mom, because she had come out to take care of her sister before she passed from cancer. Mom fell in love with the ocean and decided to stay. She has early stages of dementia, and I'm trying to talk her into coming back to Arizona with me. Meanwhile, I took this job. Too much information?"

"Nah," he laughed. "I'm from North Dakota. I followed my sister out here. I can't get used to the rain either!"

"You're Native, aren't you? Do you live on the reservation here?"

"Yes, ma'am. I'm Hidatsa and Sioux. My sister is the doc on the rez, and I stay with her. I asked you to come over here because there has been an accident, and I need help sorting some things out. Marie Harper was killed two nights ago in a car crash."

"Oh no! I am so sorry to hear that! And the baby, is she all right?"

"Yes, Heather is fine. She is in the hospital for now. I'm hoping you might be able to help me. Did Marie give you any references when she rented this apartment?"

"Yes, I've got the file with me. She had been living in Hoquiam and working for a doctor's clinic in Aberdeen. I have everything here."

Rod took the paperwork and copied it on Marie's printer. "Thanks! This is a great help. Did she happen to mention anything about her life to you, from before?"

"No, only that she was a single mother. Why the questions? Was the crash not an accident?"

"We are investigating all possibilities. The other vehicle belonged to a couple, the Wilsons. I'm wondering, does your office happen to handle their rental as well?"

"Why yes, we do. Are they okay?"

"He is. Jessica is in the hospital. I guess it won't hurt to tell you... Jimmy Wilson may be Heather's biological father. If he passes the paternity test, they are taking the baby since there is no one else. Do you remember how long they have lived here?"

"Jimmy moved into the cabin last spring. He married Jessica in February, this year, and she moved in with him. I like Jessica a lot! I eat often at the restaurant she worked at out on the highway. I remember her telling me about Jimmy's proposal, and how sweet he was about her not being able to have children." She stood looking out the window as though mesmerized by the rain. "Detective, you don't think the crash was purposeful, do you?" she looked at him, stunned by the thought.

"Like I said, we are looking into all possibilities. My office will be in touch about collecting her personal things," Rod said.

"That's fine. The house was furnished. I'll pack up her personal belongings." She put on her coat and stepped out into the drizzle.

"Here's my card if you think of anything else." Rod said.

CHAPTER THIRTEEN

Rod stopped by the Shoalwater police station, visited with the receptionist for a minute, and got the okay from Chief Winters to continue the Aberdeen investigation. Rod couldn't have asked for a better boss. Winters had been Police Chief here for over ten years, and had also done a stint as Tribal Chairman before that, as well. He was as solid as they come, both physically and emotionally. After Rod filled him in on the wreck and his suspicions, the Chief said, "Sounds like you finally got a break on this case. If you need anything from us just let me know." Rod thanked him and left. He stopped at the casino to fill his car with gas, then headed out the highway.

Back at the station in Aberdeen he started going through a box of papers he had gathered up at Marie's apartment. He had taken everything personal, including some photos and other items from her family history he thought Jessica might want to show Heather as she grew up. He hoped Jessica and Jimmy would tell her about Marie. Everyone deserves to know where they came from.

He went through Marie's bank and credit card statements for January of the previous year, hoping something would link her to Jimmy, or the other victims.

He had six piles laid out on a table: Marie's, Jimmy's, and one for each of the dead women. At the top he placed photos, which he looked at first. They had been able to get decent photos of the other four women from their families. They definitely were of a type. All were thin with long brown hair. He looked through January after January, year after year, trying to find some connection. Finally, something stood out.

He looked back at Jimmy's work history. Currently he was employed down at the docks in Westport, in a fish shack, cooking crab, filleting fish, and selling to the public. Before that he had worked at a gas station in Hoquiam. On January 10, last year, there was a charge at that same station on Marie's Visa, for gas and some snacks. He checked the credit card statements of the other four women. Two of them had charges on January 10, the year they were killed, the first victim, and the last. He would stake his life that the other two shopped there too, and paid cash on the day they were killed, which had to be January 10! *Thank you, Grandfather,* he acknowledged silently, *for helping me see this.*

Rod checked Jimmy's credit card statements and found a charge for two dinners, each January 10th, at the same restaurant; Jimmy was nothing if not consistent. Rod went to Chief Dolan with his findings.

"This is not enough to get a search warrant, Sergeant. Just because someone shopped at the place Mr. Wilson worked doesn't mean he killed them. We don't know what day they died, exactly, either. Remember, they were found in the woods, some of them months after they were killed. Two were so decomposed we couldn't tell if they had the burn marks on their chests! Go to the restaurant with their photos and see if anyone remembers them."

Rod took the four women's photos, and one of Marie that he had taken from her house and drove to downtown Aberdeen. He found the restaurant on a side street. The owner of the restaurant looked at the five photos, but couldn't say he had ever seen four of them. He remembered Marie, though. She had worked nearby and often came into the restaurant for lunch. There was only one server still working at the restaurant who had been there in January, and he didn't recognize the woman who had been killed this year. He had only been there ten months, so Rod didn't bother showing him the other photos. He needed a photo of Jimmy. He headed back to the hospital to take one.

He had spent hours last night mulling over everything he thought he knew. And the reality is he knew darn little. He had thought about the legends of Iktome, the spider, and how crafty she was, spinning that web with such patience, and cunning, to be able to trap her food each day; how, when her prey landed on the web, tearing a hole in it, she repaired the damage, making it stronger, harder for the next unlucky ones to escape. He was certain Marie was a victim who had escaped the web, and wondered if it was through her own actions, or if this Iktome had refrained from tightening the rope around her neck, allowing her to struggle out of the binding strand, and if so, why?

As he walked through the hospital lobby, he got a text from Chief Dolan. 'The paternity test came back. Jimmy is the father.' "OK, then, time to rock and roll!" He chuckled to himself as he got in the elevator, remembering the first time he had heard that expression.

It was from Mrs. H., during the Christmas pageant at school. She was in charge of it and had worked with each grade on a portion of the program. The fifth graders danced to a song, "Rockin' Around the Christmas Tree." She had taught them to jitterbug. That night one of the girls didn't show up and his cousin looked so dejected out there, with no dance partner. Mrs. H. just grabbed him and off they went. A trilling sound filled the gymnasium as the families in the bleachers all rattled their tongues, in appreciation! She didn't just dance jitterbug, either. At every powwow, wake, and other ceremonies she was out there with her shawl, dancing with his people.

He walked in on Jimmy and Jessica playing with the baby. Rod took his phone out of his jacket pocket and took their photo. "I'm going to Walgreens later. I'll make a copy for you...your first family photo," he told them.

WONDERFUL Jessica wrote on her board.

She looks happy, thought Rod. She has no idea what's coming.

"So, I just heard the good news! You are Heather's father, and that will make it easier for you to get custody. They said a social worker will come out to do a home study and wellness check after Jessica and the baby are released, then everything should be just a formality."

"Yeah, we're excited to get home and start our life with her. I was just leaving," said Jimmy. "I've been away from work for three days, but they need me back. Jessie will be here at least four more days, then her mother is coming out to stay with us for a few weeks until she gets back on her feet." He handed Heather back to Jessica then left the room just as the nurse came in to get Heather.

"Why the hell is that cop still hanging around," Jimmy worried to himself as he walked out of the building.

"Jessica," Rod started. "The nurse told me Jimmy has been telling you stories about your life. Is it helping with memory loss?" She shook her head, no. "Well, I hope when you start talking again it will help it to come back. I don't know about stuff like that, but I have a friend, a teacher of mine from high school, who studied speech therapy. She lives nearby and would like to meet you; answer any questions you might have. Would that be okay?" She nodded, yes.

He called Becky, and asked her if she was free to come to the hospital right then. He gave her the room number.

Rod sat in the chair next to the bed. "You're probably wondering why I'm still coming to visit. I can't tell you everything, but I can tell you that the woman who died, Heather's biological mother, may be connected to a case we have been working on for several years."

Jessica stared at Rod, then wrote WHAT KIND OF CASE

"It's that serial murderer that's been on the news for four years. We think Marie may be a victim that got away because of some evidence on her body."

Evidence on my body? It must be those cigarette burns. WHAT EVIDENCE

"I can't share that, because that information has not been released in any of the statements. Because of Heather's age, we think Marie may have escaped the killer around the time the baby was conceived. If Marie was involved with Jimmy, then she may have told him something about what happened to her." He watched her as she digested this news.

"It's really important that you don't say anything to Jimmy or anyone about this. The only reason I'm telling you is that you are vulnerable with your memory loss. Jimmy may have told you something Marie shared with him that might put you in danger if you remember it."

She turned and looked out the window. *I know everything that would put me in danger. If you only knew what I know. How can I tell you who I am, what he did to me? You wouldn't believe it!* BUT HE DIDN'T KILL MARIE

"No. We never would have connected her to the case if it weren't for the marks. That terrible accident, and her death, may be the key to us solving this."

She sat and mulled that over. *It has to be those burns on my chest they found. Oh my God...he didn't just rape me. He raped those other women. Why did he burn me, then leave?* That night she had begged him not to rape her, told him she could get pregnant. He had left, abruptly, after the rape and the burning. *Did he stalk me, after? Did he know I was pregnant? He told me that "we" got married in February, on Valentine's Day, and were going to adopt a baby. Did he kill me on purpose so they could have his child to themselves?*

Rod watched her face, her eyes, as they registered the thoughts she was having: surprise, shock, betrayal, and finally, some kind of recognition. *What the hell is going on in that mind of hers? It's as though she is remembering and thinking about something in the past — is that possible with amnesia?* "Jessica, if you remember anything Jimmy may have told you about Marie that might help us, please tell me immediately."

I CAN DO THAT

"Great! I'm starving. I'm going down to the cafeteria to get something to eat, then I'll be back when my friend gets here."

CHAPTER FOURTEEN

He texted Becky to meet him in the cafeteria. He was halfway through a large portion of mac and cheese when she arrived.

"Yum! Comfort food!" she said, as she hugged his shoulders and sat down.

"Want some?"

"No, thanks. I ate before I came into town. What's up?"

He filled her in on everything he had learned since yesterday, including Jimmy being the father and the strong possibility that he is the serial killer.

"And you're going to let her go home with him???"

"Legally we don't have a choice. We have no evidence. I'm hoping you will work with her on her voice and maybe get some information, or insight into her. I have a feeling she knows more than she is telling. You were always so good at that intuitive stuff. I remember the day that summer, sitting in your kitchen drinking lemonade...I wanted to spill my guts to you."

"You were going to tell me something that day, weren't you...that you were pulling the sled when the little guys went through the ice?" She reached out and touched his arm.

"Yeah." He looked up at her and saw that she knew and had not changed her feelings for him.

"It wasn't your fault. You couldn't have saved them, even if you had run and told someone. Mr. Blackstone was the one who found them the next day. It was so cold the ice had closed back up as soon as they fell through. He told me the only way he knew where to look was the sled tracks and the footprints. You need to forgive yourself. Have you given it to the Creator, when you are in the sweat lodge?"

"No. I haven't. I didn't think I deserved forgiveness. I'll make an offering and turn it over next time I'm in for a sweat."

"Good. Because they are with Him, now, and you need to be relieved of this burden. Now, what do you want me to do with this Jessica of yours?"

They went back upstairs after making a plan. Jessica was waking up from a nap as they walked in. Rod introduced them.

"I hope you don't mind that Rod has shared your story with me, Jessica. You've been through quite an ordeal. I would love to work with you as you heal from this wound and begin using your voice again. May I ask, does your throat hurt inside, or is it just painful outside, on your neck tissue?" Becky asked.

BOTH THE LEFT SIDE HURTS INSIDE AND OUT

"Well, that's reassuring. If you can feel it, it didn't paralyze the vocal cord and you'll be able to use your voice soon. Do you have any questions?

I DONT HEAR A DRAWL IN MY HEAD JIMMY SAYS I HAVE A DRAWL

Well, I didn't see that coming, thought Rod. *Why on earth would that be on her mind?*

"That's a great question!" Becky responded. "Our vocal inflections, drawls, accents, that kind of thing, are learned based on patterns we hear as we grow. They stay with us depending on how long we are exposed to them. If you still had a drawl before the accident, and hadn't lost it after moving out here, you should still have it when your voice returns. The exception is when someone has a stroke. Sometimes after a stroke, or a head trauma, a person has what is known as Foreign Accent Syndrome. They speak with an accent different from that of their native country. This is rare, but you can see instances of it if you google it. Have you tried to use your voice?"

She shook her head. DR SAID IT WOULD HEAL BETTER IF I DIDN'T SPEAK

"Well, that's true, but you could try. It will come out in a whisper, just like when you have a bad cold, or laryngitis. Do you want to try?"

WILL A WHISPER HAVE AN ACCENT

Becky laughed. "I have no idea! Want to try?" She leaned over the bed, putting her ear next to Jessie's mouth.

Jessica whispered, "Do I have an accent?" "Not that I can tell," Becky whispered back.

They both laughed. Rod watched all this with great interest. He hadn't seen Jessica this relaxed before. *Becky certainly makes her magic with everyone. Between us, we need to find out whatever secrets that girl is keeping that might get her in trouble.*

They agreed that when Jessica got home, Becky would visit, and work with her on restoring her voice.

As they walked out to their cars Becky said, "She's not going to need me, you know. Her voice will come back by itself."

"But I need you," he said. "I need you to keep an eye on her while I keep digging for more on Jimmy. Her mother will be there, but I want someone who knows the danger they are in if this goes sideways before we have enough for a warrant. Do you feel comfortable helping me with this?" he asked.

"Sure," she hugged him, "Later." "Later," he replied.

As she drove back out to Westport, she thought about that custom his tribe had, to never say good-bye, only "later." Some people who followed the traditional ways believed that saying good-bye was permanent; to say "see you later" was a good thing. The day she left the reservation, Rod and several other students had come to help pack the truck. He hugged her then, "See ya later" he said.

He had done the same thing the following year, when she went back for his graduation. She never thought she would see him again and now here they were. Funny how things work out.

Rod decided to swing by the office of the medical clinic where Marie had done transcriptions to see if he could learn anything. When he got out of the car, he noticed the restaurant Jimmy had frequented was across the street. He walked over to the restaurant, pulled out his phone, and approached the owner. "You again!" The man grinned at him.

"Yeah, I got another photo to show you. You remember this man? He may have come in with the women I showed you earlier."

"No...wait. You still have those other photos?" Rod went back to the car, got the folder, and returned. He spread the photos out on the counter. The owner took the phone and held it to each photo. He stopped at Marie's. "This woman I told you about last time. She worked across the street and ate lunch here often. Yeah...she did come in with this guy one night. I remember thinking she was way out of his league. Then she stopped coming in for lunch."

Rod thanked him and headed over to the medical clinic. He introduced himself to the receptionist and told her he had some questions about Marie Harper.

"Oh, what a tragedy, her just having that baby and all! We are just heart sick over it." shared the receptionist.

"Can you tell me when Marie stopped working here in the office and started working from home?" Rod asked.

"Of course. Let me get her file." She went to a cabinet, pulled out a folder and opened it between them. "Here it is. She told us she was pregnant and going to move back in with her mother, in Hoquiam, and wanted to work remotely. That was approved and her last day at the office was February 3, last year. She stopped in again in March, after her mother died of a heart attack. She had found a place out in Tokeland and wanted to keep working remotely, which was approved."

"Thank you. That helps a lot," and he left.

So, she may have had dinner at the restaurant with Jimmy the night she got pregnant. Timing fits. It doesn't prove it was a rape. The killer could have raped her, around that time, but why let her go? he thought as he got back in the car. He decided to drive through and get a burger, then head back to the station to see if Carmen had found out anything about Jimmy's past.

CHAPTER FIFTEEN

Jimmy had just gotten off work, went home to clean up, and headed for the hospital. When he walked into Jessie's room, she was holding Heather, an empty bottle on the tray table next to her. "My two beautiful girls!" he said, sitting on the bed with them.

This doesn't even seem like the guy I went out with. Maybe he has a twin. Nah...they wouldn't have the same name.

She handed him the baby and picked up the whiteboard. TELL ME SOMETHING ABOUT YOU THAT YOU ALREADY TOLD ME MAYBE THAT WILL HELP ME REMEMBER

"There is not a lot to tell. I never knew my dad. My mom raised me right here in Aberdeen. I barely graduated high school. I've had a series of dead-end jobs until I got this one. It's messy and stinky, but I think I can get hired on with one of the fishing boats we buy from. That's my dream! I love being on the water. I talked to one of the guys that owns a boat, Dick Fischer is his name. Funny, huh? Fischer, and he is a fisher. He's here crabbing right now, but he's leaving for Alaska in a few weeks, for the salmon run. He needs a deckhand. I worked on engines a lot growing up, and he said I could help the engineer too, and learn that. It's a terrific opportunity, Jessie, but it would mean leaving you and the baby for the summer." He had Heather sitting on his knees, facing him. He started playing patty-cake with her, which brought out peals of laughter.

Yes! Leave! That would solve a lot of problems! Boy, she sure does look like you.

MOM WILL BE HERE   IT WOULD BE A FRESH START

It will get you out of here while I figure out how to live this lie, and give Sergeant Kills On Top time to figure out if you are living one too.

"It will mean more money. We'll need that with the baby. You won't be able to go back to work at the restaurant for a while. Do you even remember how to be a waitress?"

I WANT TO WORK FROM HOME SO I CAN STAY WITH HEATHER.

"Really? You can do that? What kind of work?"

MEDICAL CODING. She watched him, to see if he had a reaction. She had told him the night he raped her that she worked for the clinic, across the street from the restaurant, transcribing patient data. He had no reaction. Nothing.

"That sounds great! We would both have new work to support our family. Do you have to go to school for that?"

THERE ARE ONLINE SCHOOLS *I'm getting stuck in the weeds, here...need to change the subject. HOW IS YOUR TRUCK*

"It's in the shop and will be ready late next week. Do you want to see the pictures I took of it?"

Do I want to see photos of the accident that killed me and messed up Jessie's body? Oh, sure. She nodded.

He took out his phone and handed it to her. She swiped through the pictures, noting the giant hole in the window, and all the blood on the front passenger seat. The last photo was her car. She gasped, looking at the twisted wreckage.

No wonder I died. How did Heather survive that without a scratch? Having her on the other side, her car seat hooked in backwards, must have saved her. That's the only part of the car that is recognizable.

She looked up at Jimmy, her eyes filled with tears, and handed back his phone.

"That detective told me there is a reason for everything, and that out of every bad thing something good comes. I never thought about that before but I believe it now. If I had known Marie was pregnant, I would have married her. She kept it from me. Now she's gone and we have the baby. Who knows, maybe Marie would have gotten sick or something and died, and Heather would have gone into foster care. Maybe this is a good thing."

Or maybe if you hadn't raped me, I never would have been pregnant, moved to Tokeland, been in that rainstorm, and got killed by you! Maybe I would still be alive, working, meeting some nice guy, getting married, and then having Heather. Maybe???

I NEED A NAP She rolled over, covered her head, and sobbed silently.

CHAPTER SIXTEEN

Carmen had Jimmy's history ready for Rod when he got back, and it wasn't good.

Jimmy had been born in Seattle, to a prostitute who worked on Aurora Avenue, between Green Lake and the cemetery, mostly. There were a lot of sleazy motels along that strip and she was known in all of them. Jimmy had been taken away from her several times, put into foster care, then returned, whenever she proved she had a decent apartment and food to feed him. "Reuniting" they called it.

Rod shook his head, thinking about the kids he had known growing up, who happened to be born into crappy families. He believed kids should be raised by their own, but too often the parents were incapable of loving and providing for their kids, because of drugs, alcoholism, whatever. It got worse with each generation. Thankfully, on the reservation, there were usually relatives that could take the kids when they needed care.

He read one of the reports and stopped to think about it. When he was six, Jimmy had been found by a neighbor, with multiple contusions and a broken arm. Jimmy said that he had fallen down the apartment steps. The neighbor had found him at the bottom of the steps, all right, but was sure Jimmy had been thrown out the window, which was open, and the frame broken. He called the ambulance, then the landlord, who went up to the apartment to find Jimmy's mom. She was drunk in bed.

The police report said they were sure he had been thrown out the window, because a piece of his flannel shirt was caught in the window frame. When they talked to Jimmy about it, he finally told the truth. He had been hungry, and stole some money from the pocket of whatever guy was in bed with his mom. He went to the store down the street, bought some food, and was eating it when the guy woke up. When the man discovered the missing money, he picked Jimmy up and threw him out the window. Jimmy didn't know that what the man had done to him was a crime. He was afraid that he himself was in trouble; that he would go to jail for stealing.

He was ten before he was taken away from his mother again, this time permanently. He had been out of school for several days, during a January storm, and the truant officer did a home check. He found Jimmy on the couch, freezing, unresponsive.

The officer covered Jimmy with a blanket and waited for the ambulance to arrive. When the paramedics tried to pick him up, Jimmy screamed. They cut off his bloody shirt to see what the damage was, and the truant officer puked. There were cigarette burns all over his back, many of them old, several recent. The burns stood out on his back like a message on a T-shirt: MOMMYS LITTLE BASTARD

Police learned from the landlord that the rent hadn't been paid for two months. He had entered the apartment three days ago, found no one there, and left a notice of eviction. The heat had been shut off two days before. They never found Jimmy's mother.

The medical exam revealed a break in his other arm that had been set at a different hospital, two fingers that had been broken and never set, and his nose had been broken. They had to sedate him to learn that he had been sexually violated, as well.

Jimmy had been placed in a group home for boys who had been abused badly, a place where, hopefully, he might be able to recover. Physical mending was the easier part. Emotional and mental healing was another issue. Would he ever be able to take his place in society as a contributing member, after a beginning like that, was the question.

According to the reports Jimmy did not form a trusting relationship with any of the adults at the home. He didn't relate well with the other boys, either, staying to himself most of the time. He attended school and did his homework. There were instances of theft occasionally, and the items were found in Jimmy's closet — cigarettes, matches, and clothesline rope from the laundry poles outside. Jimmy had cut a piece off the rope and was using it as a belt. Adults learned to keep their smokes and matches hidden. When questioned, Jimmy said he didn't know why he took them, that he felt he had to. Other times he said he didn't remember doing it at all. He also woke often in the night, with panic attacks. They would find him hiding in the closet.

The therapist who worked with him assured the adults who worked there that he was not stealing so he could smoke. She felt he was doing it to prevent someone from burning him. The clothesline she couldn't find a reason for, and when she talked to him about it, he shut down, staring in front of him, as though the answer might be there, in the air.

Rod read through several more pages, learning that Jimmy never recovered fully enough to go into foster care. He stayed in the group home until he was discharged at eighteen. He had finished school and was able to hold down part-time jobs for the last two years. There was one bizarre incident noted in his file during January of his last year there.

The owner of the convenience store where Jimmy worked stocking shelves after school, called the group home to report that Jimmy had walked off the job that evening. He had been filling the pop cooler near the checkout stand when a woman came in and bought cigarettes. Jimmy had stood staring at her, then followed her out of the store. The owner went out to look but couldn't tell which way he had gone.

The report stated that Jimmy came back to the group home late that night, wet, cold, and without his jacket or his rope belt. His palms were chafed, as though trying to keep something from slipping through his fingers. He told them he didn't know where he had been or what he had been doing. In a session the next day he told the therapist that he thought he had been watching himself, in an alley, covering something up on the ground, and then he was back at the home. He was confused and anxious, and she believed he didn't remember.

Rod checked the date of Jimmy's disappearance — January 10, 2013. Five years ago... one year before the first body turned up on the reservation. He sat there shaking his head, hating where this was leading him. He asked Charlotte to contact the Seattle Police Department and see if there were any female homicide cold cases that day, near Aurora, then he headed home for the night. He called P.J. and asked him to get the sweat ready. Then he called Becky to see if she wanted to go in with him. He said he would pick her up on his way through Westport.

CHAPTER SEVENTEEN

Becky's little place was tidy and filled with mementos from her travels. He noticed her abalone shell with a sage stick in it on top of the bookcase. Next to it were the fan she had carried during the Sun Dance, and a clay pot filled with dried corn-on-the-cob. "Is that original corn?" he asked in amazement.

"Yes, it is. I was gifted that, along with two eagle feathers, by Superintendent Lone Wolf when I left Mandaree."

"I remember, he had the right to give feathers away. That right was passed down to him by his grandfather."

Becky had changed into her sweat dress and was packing a bag with her towel and clothes. "What do you mean, right to give them?"

"In our way, only people who have been given the right can give an eagle feather to another person — unless an eagle gives it to you! Is that one of your Sun Dance dresses? It's beautiful!"

"Yes. I made it myself. The ribbons are a bit tattered. I wore it for three years, in North Dakota. Since then, I've worn it in the lodge.

It's been a few years since I went for a sweat. I'm looking forward to it," Becky answered.

On the way out to his place he filled her in on what he had learned about Jimmy's past.

"I'm astounded that he is able to carry on a normal life at all." she said. "What you are describing to me points to a condition called Dissociative Identity Disorder. It used to be known as multiple personality disorder, but they've learned so much about the brain and how it can departmentalize and have recognized so many other symptoms attached to it, that they have renamed it."

"How do you know about this?" Rod asked.

"The last two years I taught I worked with children with special needs. We had a nine-year-old boy who was showing signs of this. We found out he was being traumatized by his stepfather, including sexual abuse. I studied the disorder so I would know how to work with him in the classroom and assist in his therapy. What are you leaning towards?"

"I'm almost certain that we're going to learn that Jimmy's mother was found killed near that store where he worked. I believe that was her who came in on January 10th that year and bought cigarettes. If it was her who burned Jimmy, maybe that set him off."

Becky continued, "That would fit with dissociation. It is often triggered by a repressed traumatic event that happened in the past. The personality splits itself to protect the innocent child from remember-ing. When triggered, the other personality takes dominance and acts out. Sometimes one of the personalities has memories of the other. Sometimes they don't and act totally separately, neither one having any idea what's happening. They lose time because of it."

Rod slammed his hand on the steering wheel. "That would explain why Jimmy didn't know where he had been that night. He showed up later, disoriented, frightened, and with no memory, except he said he thought he was watching himself cover something up in an alley."

"People with this disorder often say they feel like they are outside their body, watching what is going on! Rod, I think we're on to something here!"

"Becky, I have to be careful here, what I tell you. I've probably shared too much already."

"You're working with the Aberdeen police, right? Can't you use me as a consultant? I have a psychology minor and have studied this disorder extensively."

He pulled into the space in front of Sam's garage. "Let me check with the Chief. Here we are, and there is someone who will be very happy to see you!"

She got out of the car and was immediately body slammed by Samantha, embraced in a hug so tight she dropped her bag. They stood in that hug, savoring the moment, until Sam stepped back, grinning. "Hey, Mrs. H! When Rod told me he ran into you on the beach I couldn't believe it. You're really here!"

"I really am, and I'm so happy to find you two. Call me Becky, okay? You look wonderful!"

"When he told me you live here, I knew it was no accident...it was meant, innit?"

"I agree, Sweetie. We were meant to find each other again. I need family around me, and I definitely met Rod at the right time to help with his case."

"Yup, it was meant! And we need family too. P.J. has the rocks ready. Let's go in." Sam led the way to the sweat lodge.

During the healing round, when Rod poured the water over the rocks, Sam sang his spirit song, the one given to him by his grandfather, and the rocks sent steam so hot Becky felt like her face was on fire. She knew it was for Rod, this heat, as he prayed, "Grandfather, Grandmother, this is Walks with Bears here in the lodge, talking to you..." and there, in the hot, steamy dark, he cried, releasing the burden of guilt he had carried all these years.

Becky prayed to be guided in the right way in her assistance with Rod's case; that she recognizes the signs that would lead to answers.

It was a balmy, late April evening, one of those rare, warm spring nights. They decided to eat outside, on a picnic table Sam had set up under the cedars. It was a crescent moon, and off the bottom tip Venus squatted in the sky. Rod missed the North Dakota skies, where one could see the entire view, in a circle. Here, with all the tall trees, the sky had a peek-a-boo effect, showing off its sparkles among the cedars.

"Who made this delicious cornbread? It's the best I've ever tasted!" exclaimed Becky.

"That would be me," P.J. said, modestly. "My Grandmother taught me to cook. I made buffalo soup too. We always made it with beef, but Sam convinced us to try buffalo and we switched."

"Tastes perfect! The only thing missing is wojapi."

"What's that?" asked P.J.

"It's a kind of soup, made with chokecherries. Sweet, and delicious," shared Sam.

"I make it with blueberries, since you can't get chokecherries here," said Becky. "I'll bring some next time."

As he drove Becky home, Rod shared his worry about Jessica. "I don't see her improving in either problem she has right now. She isn't remembering anything and she is not speaking yet, not even trying. I watch her around Jimmy and there is definitely something she is afraid of. I noticed it the first time she opened her eyes and saw him there in the room. There's something just not right."

"Do you know when she is being released from the hospital?"

"Yeah, the day after tomorrow, if all goes well with her check-up with Dr. Singh. Her mother is coming in from Kentucky to Seattle on an evening flight. She's taking the Airporter to Olympia and Jimmy is picking her up there and bringing her back to his place. He's working tomorrow. Do you think you could go in and talk to her, and make arrangements to work with her when she comes home?"

"Sure. I was going to town anyway to get groceries. I'll ask her what she wants and shop for them. That will give me an excuse to go over to the house and sniff around."

Rod laughed. "You sound just like a cop."

"I watch a lot of crime shows on TV! Really, Rod, I want to help with this as much as I can. Her mom is going to be here for a bit, but Jessie will need help after she leaves."

"I agree. I'll be in the office tomorrow, finding out what Carmen learned about the night Jimmy disappeared. Let's meet for lunch after you've visited her, so we can share what we learn and make a plan."

CHAPTER EIGHTEEN

The next morning Rod checked with Chief Dolan regarding using Becky as a consultant. "She wants to help, and she doesn't want to be paid. I know her and trust her. What she told me already about that disorder makes sense."

"Yes, it does. Let me give it some thought. I don't want to put a private citizen in danger. If you can find a way for her to work with Jessie without Jimmy being involved, that would be ideal. Now, go talk to Carmen. She's been waiting to share something with you."

He grabbed a coffee, went to Carmen's cubicle, and plunked himself on a chair next to her desk. "Hey, whatcha got?"

"You were right to connect Jimmy's disappearance with a possible killing. Seattle PD has a cold case from that night. A body was found in an alley two blocks from the store where Jimmy worked. They identified her from prints they had when she was arrested for prostitution. It was Georgia Wilson, Jimmy's mother. They assumed it was a customer who killed her, but there was no evidence of sexual encounter."

He dropped his face into his hands. "Crap, crap and more crap. I was hoping that wouldn't be the case. If there was no sexual assault it was probably Jimmy, but it makes it harder to prove. Give me the details."

"She was strangled with a piece of clothesline rope. During the autopsy they found one burn mark on each breast, the size of a cigarette. The package of cigarettes she had purchased was placed between her breasts. Two cigarettes were gone — one she was smoking which they found on the ground, and another, which was probably used to burn her, and was not recovered. Oh, one other thing. After he finished with her, the killer placed his coat over her torso and face. I remember reading in Jimmy's file, that he got back to the group home that night without his jacket."

"I wonder why it was not reported to the case worker who had placed Jimmy at the group home. There was nothing in his file about her death."

"You know how much paperwork there is in these cases. Maybe they didn't search far enough to find out about Jimmy," Carmen answered, as she watched him process this new information.

Rod thought about the Jimmy he knew, rough around the edges, but caring of Jessica and the baby. Was it possible that he had two identities, the caring one who is so happy to be a father, and another deviant one, capable of the brutal acts that had been perpetrated on these women? Jimmy's mother was strangled with clothesline rope, as were the victims from Aberdeen.

He opened the file again, looking through it for anything he may have missed. When he got to the part about Jimmy being found outside the apartment after being thrown out the window, he decided to call the apartment owner to see if he could remember anything that would help.

"Yeah, Mr. Delaney, this is Sergeant Kills On Top, calling from Aberdeen, on a police matter concerning a family that lived in your building a few years ago."

"What did you say your name was?"

"Sergeant Kills On Top."

"That's what I thought you said. Huh! What can I help you with?"

"Do you remember Georgia and Jimmy Wilson? They lived in Apartment 204."

"Hell, yeah, I remember them. She was a psycho. Always screaming at the kid and beating him too, they found out. He was a mess the day they took him away from her."

"I'm wondering if you can remember anything, anything at all, about the apartment the day that happened. I understand you evicted her. Did you find anything odd at all?"

"The place was a mess. I had to hire someone to come in and clean. There was one thing that was really strange. It looked like the kid had been sleeping in the closet. Attached to the back wall was an eye bolt with a long piece of clothesline tied to it. It had what looked like dried blood on it."

"Did you report that to the police?"

"Nah. They had taken the kid away and the mother had disappeared, so I didn't bother."

"Thanks, Mr. Delaney. I appreciate your help. Oh, by the way...do you remember what the mom looked like?" There was a pause, then, "Yeah. She was a skinny little piece of work with long brown hair."

Rod gave him his phone number in case he thought of anything else. But he knew that was enough. Jimmy had been held captive in the closet, tied up with rope. Rod bet it was while she had her johns with her in the apartment. She hid Jimmy away, probably gagged him too. He was sure it was blood on the rope, from Jimmy trying to escape. He was also sure the clothesline he had stolen at the group home, and wore as a belt, was what he used to kill his mother. The report said he did not have it on him when he returned the next day.

He stood outside the Chief's office, staring at her, until she looked up. Seeing the look on his face, she motioned him in, and fixed him a cup of coffee.

"What is that thing you use to make your coffee?" he asked.

"It's a French Press. I grind the beans, organic, from Guatemala. I like the flavor and making it a couple of cups at a time. It's a meditative process." she smiled.

"Yeah, well, I need a meditative process right now. My mind is screaming."

"What's up?"

He told her about the phone call with the apartment owner, and his conclusions.

"Rod, it looks like you have your killer, but there is really nothing to tie him to the murders at all. We need something to connect him, other than that they shopped where he worked. Do you want to question him at this point?"

"No! If he has two people living in him, I sure don't want to poke the bear. If I bring the Jimmy I know in, the other one may pop out later and hurt Jessica. I need to think this through. I'm meeting Becky for lunch. I'll talk to her about the personality thing and get back to you."

"OK, just be careful how much you bring Becky into this." she warned.

Rod went back to his cubicle, to the whiteboard, and began laying out all the facts he now had, looking for something to go on, some piece of evidence to follow, some hunch.

CHAPTER NINETEEN

Becky had come into town early, planning on stopping by the hospital before she met Rod for lunch and did her shopping. She walked into Jessica's room, just as she was playing the mouse game with Heather. Jessica was running her fingers up and down the baby's arms as she sang, in a whispery voice, "There once was a mouse who had a wee house, and went creepy crawly, creepy crawly all the way home!"

"Well, look at you two! What a beautiful baby you have, Jessica! And it sounds like your voice is coming back!"

"A little," Jessica whispered.

"Wonderful! And I hear your mom is coming in tonight, and you get to go home tomorrow? I would love to start working on the recovery of your voice."

Jessica handed Heather to Becky when she reached out for her. I HAVE NO DRAWL she wrote.

"Yes, I noticed!" Becky said, smiling. "Why is that a problem?" She began bouncing Heather on her knee, and the baby laughed. "She really is a happy baby, and was obviously well cared for and loved," she said, while Jessica wrote.

JIMMY LIKES MY DRAWL WHAT IF HE GETS MAD OR THINKS I'M NOT ME

"Well, maybe it has something to do with your memory loss. I told you about that rare thing called Foreign Accent Syndrome. Maybe it's related to that, somehow. You've been through a lot, Jessica, and I wouldn't worry about it. If it bothers you, I can talk to Jimmy about it." *Why is she so obsessed about this, and why would she even think he would question if she is herself,* Becky wondered? *And, more importantly, why doesn't she have a drawl?*

YES PLEASE HE'LL PICK ME UP IN THE MORNING CAN YOU COME

"I was hoping you would let me do some shopping for you today. I can pick up some food and other items you will need for your mom to cook for you, and whatever you need for Heather. I can bring them to your house tomorrow. Try your voice again."

Jessica whispered, "Thanks, that would be great! Jimmy leaves on a fishing boat tomorrow for Blaine, then on to Alaska."

"Well, that helps with the drawl issue — don't talk to Jimmy before he leaves! Keep using the whiteboard. We'll figure out the answer while he's gone. It will also give you time with your mom, and to get settled into life again, with Heather. I'm going to have lunch with Sergeant Kills On Top. Why don't you make a grocery list while I do that and I'll swing back by and pick it up." She gave Jessica a quick hug and left. *That's good news,* she mused as she got in the elevator. *That will get him out of town while Rod completes his investigation. And I can spend time with her and maybe she will confide in me about what's really bothering her.*

Becky met Rod at a Thai place they both liked. He was there when she arrived, and already had Thai iced tea for both. "My favorite drink, besides coffee!" She said as she slid into the booth. "I just came from the hospital. Jessica told me that Jimmy is leaving Monday for Blaine, on a fishing boat, to get ready for the salmon season. And, she does not have an accent, which is very weird!"

"That makes my job a lot easier if he'll be out of the picture while I put this case together. I'm going to go by the hospital tomorrow to give them a photo I took of the three of them."

"And I'm going to shop for her today and take it by the house tomorrow. Do you have their address?"

"I do. I'll text it to you when I'm back at the office." He explained to her what they had learned about Jimmy's mother's death, and the clothesline rope in the closet.

"Dang...that about ties it up — no pun intended!"

"Yeah, but it really doesn't. We have no proof yet. I have this gut feeling that Jessica is a key to what we need, somehow, but I can't put it together. She is definitely afraid of Jimmy, yet when they are together, I see her opening up to him."

"Isn't that common with abusers and their spouses, how the wife is always hopeful that it won't happen again?"

"Maybe that's it. Maybe his dark side has come out in the marriage, some, and she is reacting. But if her memory is gone, how would she know?" Rod pondered.

"I hadn't thought of that. You're right. She wouldn't. He would just be another stranger to her, like you and me."

"She is definitely afraid of something. I can't question her because trust hasn't been built. You can do that, Becky, build trust with her. When you drop off the groceries tomorrow, be as kind to Jimmy as possible and assure him you will keep working with Jessica on her voice. Then leave. Don't go back until he's gone."

"The thing that's bothering me is her voice," shared Becky. "She has no drawl. She should have a drawl. Jimmy says she does, and she is worried about it. I've read about people who have a foreign accent after a stroke, but I can't find anything on a person losing an accent!"

"If a person develops a foreign accent, don't they lose their own, whatever it is?"

Becky thought about it. "Well, I guess they do! Maybe, in this case, the accent she developed was from here. Maybe she had a TIA, a mini stroke, that caused it."

"Well, that makes sense, sort of. If it's a mini stroke maybe it chooses an accent close by, rather than across the ocean, like a huge stroke." She looked at him shaking her head, and they both laughed, getting relief from the stressful conversation.

They finished their meal, then went their separate ways, he to the station, and she back to the hospital to pick up Jessica's grocery list.

CHAPTER TWENTY

After shopping, Becky went back out to Westport, dropped off the groceries, then went over to Judy's for a visit. She was getting ready for a walk on the beach. Becky grabbed a leash, attached it to Beatrice, while Judy tethered Luna, and off they went.

As they walked, Becky shared her dilemma about the drawl with Judy, who had studied linguistics.

"You know, the indigenous people of Guatemala have over twenty dialects of the Mayan language — in a country the size of Tennessee!" Judy shared. "Until a few decades ago, because the country is so mountainous, many of the people didn't know the others existed. After tunnels were built through the mountains, they learned of each other. Their language had been spoken since the original Mayan people.

These descendants speak variations of it, Mam, Q'anjob'al, Cakchiquel, K'iche and more. They don't understand the others. There are similarities in the way sounds are made, and in intonation, but the languages are different. If you think about the United States, it's similar. Although we all speak English, it sounds different in other regions of the country. The southern drawl is different depending on which state you are in."

"People who grew up on reservations seem to have an intonation that's totally unique too!" shared Becky. "My friend lived most of his life off the reservation, so doesn't have such a distinguished speech pattern, but he still has the language and vocabulary he learned there." She stopped and got her camera out to take photos of jellyfish that had come in during the night and were stranded on the beach, hundreds of them. They were a beautiful turquoise blue, with a little transparent sail on top. "What are those?" she exclaimed.

"They're called Vela Velas. They can't survive until the next high tide, so they die here on the beach. Part of the circle of life."

The wind had picked up, so they turned around and started back up the beach.

"My point in telling you about the Guatemalans, is that spoken language is critical to the development of a society. Wherever you are born, you will pick up the language spoken there, in whatever form. You don't know you are speaking any differently from others until you are exposed to another language, or a different speech pattern in your own language. Like your friend, who moved off the reservation and picked up intonations from the outside, Jessica has lived in Washington long enough to have learned the speech patterns here. Perhaps, somehow, those patterns, stored in her brain, took precedence over her Kentucky drawl during this trauma. Maybe the surgery she had for that birth defect exacerbated it. Or maybe it was a TIA."

"Thanks! I can explain all of that to them tomorrow when I take their groceries to them."

Judy thought for a minute. "I would love to meet her sometime. After her mother leaves you can bring her and the baby over for lunch."

"Sounds like a plan." They stood and watched as Luna, her black standard poodle, ran up to a group of people on the beach, waiting to be petted. Becky laughed. "She is such a friendly dog!"

"She does that with everyone! I know more people because of that dog, than I have met on my own!"

They climbed back up the dunes, hugged goodbye, then Becky got in her car and drove home.

CHAPTER TWENTY-ONE

Becky made herself coffee, sat down at her laptop, and decided to go online and do some more research on DID. She found an article, *Everything You Need to Know About Dissociative Identity Disorder*, from HealthPrep.

As she read, she copied the main points to share with Rod, the sections especially pertinent to Jimmy.

Dissociative Identity Disorder, also known as DID, used to be referred to as Multiple Personality Disorder. It is a condition in which the affected individual has a minimum of two distinct and enduring personalities.

Depersonalization is when the individual feels like they are watching their lives from the outside, almost like an out of body experience.

Dissociative disorders are the result of trauma, emerging as a coping mechanism to deal with the stress caused by it. It can go undiagnosed until adulthood, but when a child is exposed to an extended period of abuse and neglect, this is when this mental illness typically starts to develop. It protects the individual's consciousness from the events they experience, so children can escape from this experience and block the memories of this abuse. In severe cases, this dissociation can result in an individual developing more than one personality.

Holy moly frijoles, Becky thought, as she digested all that she had read. She was convinced Jimmy had DID and had acted out on these women without his main personality being aware of it. Given how well adjusted he seemed, she was pretty sure that his subordinate personality, the killer, was aware of innocent Jimmy, and took control whenever he was needed for Jimmy's protection. She called Rod. "Can you talk for a minute?"

"Sure. I'm in the car, on my way back home. What's up?"

"I'm emailing you a copy of the research I did online today, on DID. I'm sure Jimmy has this disorder, and that his dark personality is aware of normal Jimmy and comes out to protect him. We must be careful not to set him off tomorrow or let him know we suspect anything. If I'm right, he will leave for this fishing trip feeling okay about everything. We don't want him to feel afraid of leaving Jessica behind without him."

The next morning, Saturday, Rod walked into the hospital room just after Jimmy and Deloris, Jessica's mom, got there. He handed the photo he had taken of their little family to Jimmy, saying, "I heard you were leaving Monday and didn't want you to go without this! I just came by to wish you good luck on your new job and tell you that I will ask the Creator for your safe return every time I'm in the sweat lodge."

"Thanks, man! I don't know what that lodge thing is, but I appreciate all the good thoughts I can get!"

"No problem. I'm happy this all turned out so well. The coroner called me this morning. When they did Marie Harper's autopsy, they discovered that she had Stage 4 uterine cancer that had metastasized. She would likely have been dead in months. Jimmy, if that wreck hadn't happened, Heather may have ended up in foster care."

The room grew silent as each person thought about that.

Jessica: *I would have been dead anyway? God, was this your way of protecting my baby, and making sure I could raise her?*

Jimmy: *I was right! I thought there was a reason for this all happening. Now Jessie and me can raise our baby and Marie won't suffer. And I don't feel guilty anymore about the crash.*

Deloris: *Such a tragic situation...but so good for everyone in the end. My daughter is rid of her headaches, and has a baby, and that poor woman didn't suffer wondering what would become of her child.*

"Well, y'all, this is a miracle all around if you ask me! The Lord works in mysterious ways and this sure proves it!" exclaimed Deloris. "Now, let's get a move on. I want to get my girl and my granddaughter home and settled in and get to know my son-in-law better before he leaves!"

Rod helped carry Jessica's flowers and other items as they made their way to the parking lot. He wished them all well, got in his car and left. He called Becky. "They just left the hospital. Jimmy is in a good mood. I'll text you the address. They should be home in about forty-five minutes."

"Great! I'll go over in an hour with their groceries and assure Jimmy that I will work with Jessica on her voice. I have a gift I picked up for Heather."

"That's very kind of you, Becky. I'm so grateful you are back in our lives. Just be careful when you are over there. Let me know if anything feels wrong."

"I will, Rod. I'll call you as soon as I leave, to let you know how it went."

"I have a better idea. There's a powwow at the tribal center. People from tribes all over will be there to celebrate the first salmon. Come by the house at about noon and go with us."

"I'd love to! See you then."

She wandered into the bedroom, opened her cedar chest and took out a burgundy shawl, embroidered with roses along the edge. It had been a gift to her from Willow, a young Suquamish girl who had been in North Dakota for a Sun Dance. She had needed a ride back to Washington. Becky was going out to visit family and friends for the summer, so she gave her a ride, and they shared the driving. This was her favorite shawl. With long fringe all around the edge, it swished and swayed beautifully as she danced. After her shower, she dressed in jeans and a long-sleeved tee shirt, put on her boots, and some beaded earrings, and pulled her hair back with a beaded barrette.

She took Jessica's perishables from the fridge and loaded everything in the car. Rod had also told her where Marie had lived, and she drove by that apartment complex on her way to Jimmy and Jessica's. How very strange life is, she thought. What are the odds the universe would place these two families so close to each other? It was as though it had been orchestrated, that they had all been put there in order for the crash to happen and for Heather to get a family before her mother died.

The horror of Jimmy's past and the things his alter had done, though, how would all of this play out? It was only a matter of time before it would all be revealed and they would have to confront him. She hoped it would go down in a good way.

The little cottage Jimmy and Jessica were renting was so cute! These beach houses were all small, but cozy. She loved the one she had bought and couldn't wait to see the inside of this one. As she hauled the totes up onto the porch the door opened.

"Here, let me help you," Jimmy said. "This was nice of you to shop for us. How much do I owe you?"

Becky gave him the receipt and he counted out the cash into her hand. "Jimmy, I want you to know I will spend as much time with Jessica as she needs to help her recover her voice. I miss my work, and this will give me something to do so I feel useful again!"

"Well, I don't know how much you charge..."

"There is no charge! This will be good for both of us, believe me. When something is done with love, there is always time, and it's never any trouble. I am alone out here, except for my friend, Judy, and I welcome the opportunity to get to know Jessica."

Jimmy said, "I thought you were friends with the detective."

"Of course, but he and his sister are more like family to me. I've known them since they were in high school."

"Really? Oh, that's cool! So, you don't just work with him on cases?"

"Oh, no! We just found each other again, after years, and he mentioned Jessie's voice and asked me to help her. That's all." She watched him as he absorbed that, and he seemed to be relieved.

"OK then. Thanks for the help!"

Becky took her gift out of the tote and went into the living room where Jessica sat with her mom, who was holding Heather. The baby looked content.

"Hi! I'm Becky Farmer, a new friend of Jessica's. I'm going to work with her as she recovers her voice."

"Pleased to meetcha. I'm Deloris Wagner, Jessica's mother." Becky smiled at the honeyed accent of Deloris's words.

"Jessica, I brought this for you and Heather, and Jimmy, this one's for you and your little girl!" Becky said as she handed out the gifts. Jimmy opened his first and found a set of bath toys with a fishing boat included. "When you get home, she should be a good age to play with these," Becky said.

"Thanks so much, Becky!" He looked genuinely pleased.

THIS WAS MY FAVORITE BOOK Jessica wrote on the whiteboard. She was holding a copy of *GOOD NIGHT MOON*. She looked at the others, a set of board books called Baby's First Library. THANK YOU BECKY

"You are very welcome. Jessica, shall I come by on Monday at about 3:00?"

She nodded and gave Becky a hug before she left.

CHAPTER TWENTY-TWO

Becky arrived at Samantha's just before noon. She let herself into the kitchen and stopped, sniffing the aroma of fresh fry bread. On the table were cardboard boxes full of it.

"Don't tell me you are making Indian tacos?"

"Yup. I made the bread and P.J. has all the fixings. The money we make will be donated to the tribe for the child development center, for new materials."

"I will certainly make a contribution to that!" Becky turned as Rod came into the room, his hair down and wet from his shower. He pulled a chair in front of her and said, "Will you, please?" She sorted his hair into three parts and began to braid it. When she got to the end, she asked for a tie to finish it. Sam, her hands in the fry bread dough, used her lips to point to a shelf in a cupboard across the room. Becky grinned. She hadn't seen anyone do that for ages. She opened the cupboard, found a hair tie in a jar, and finished off the braid.

"Thanks! Time to rock and roll!" He grinned. Becky laughed, remembering how he learned that phrase. They all piled into his car and drove to the Tribal Center, where the powwow was being held in the gym.

They could hear the beat of the drum from the parking lot. Everyone was on the beach for the salmon ceremony. They walked down and listened to the speech and prayers for a good, safe salmon season.

As they entered the gym they saw the singers in the far corner, six guys sitting around the big drum, each with a drumstick, keeping the rhythm of the song they sang. She didn't recognize the language. Must be one of the tribes from up the coast. There were four more drums set up around the gym. At one she saw singers from the Lummi Nation and the Nooksack people.

She had worked for the Nooksacks years ago, in their Head Start program. She wandered over and introduced herself. "I worked with an elder named Rose. Do any of you know her?"

A man in his late thirties stood up. "That would be my grandma. She's gone now, to the spirit world. I remember you. You taught me and my sister, Rosemary." He shook her hand. "Please give my love to your sister, and anyone else who may remember me," she asked, then left to find Rod.

He was standing behind another drum speaking with the singers there. She recognized the sign in front of the drum, from the Lakota people. He motioned her over with his head and introduced them to her.

Just then the flag bearers stepped onto the floor and behind them the dancers. As the drum thrummed in the air, and the singers belted out a song, the dancers followed the flags, in a circle, clockwise, around the gym. Becky watched, enraptured. She never tired of the beauty of this procession. As they passed, she and Rod stepped into the end of the line of dancers, joining the circle. Quickly her feet found the rhythm, and she stepped lightly, toe first, then heel, step by step, her shawl over her shoulders, arms tucked in, holding it in front of her, as she moved to the beat of the drum.

When the opening procession was over she went to find Samantha in the hall where the food was being served. For the next two hours she spread cooked hamburger, spiced with taco seasoning, over pieces of fry bread, passing it to P.J. to add the tomatoes, lettuce, onion and cheese. Tubs of salsa were at the end of the table, along with napkins and plastic forks. Every fifteen minutes or so Sam would take her spot so she could go watch the dance contests. She loved the ladies' fancy and traditional dances.

She and Rod took part in the friendship dance, and finally, her favorite, the owl dance, which is the only partner dance. "You sure do remember these steps well, Becky. I'm impressed!"

"Rod, living with your people was a highlight of my life in many ways. I haven't forgotten anything!" They went over and stood behind the drum with the Lakota people, and sang the songs they knew with them.

When the tacos had all been sold, Sam and P.J. came into the gym and danced during an open round. Then they packed up and drifted out into the night, with the others who left early. They had made almost $500 for the preschool program!

As they drove home, Sam teased Becky. "My Auntie called today. When I told her you were coming to the powwow she said not to let you near the computers where they score the dancers. I asked why and she just laughed so hard. She said to make you tell me. I'm thinking you did something crazy and I can hold it over you! "

"Wow, that's a memory I'd rather forget," Becky laughed. "The first summer I was with you all I went to the powwow with your family. Your Auntie took me upstairs, to the loft over the dance arena, and asked me to help her record the dancers' scores. She showed me how to do it and I put the scores in the computer for the women's traditional dancers, as they came in from the judges. The scores were really close. When they wanted the two top scores for the dance-off I gave them to her. She couldn't believe it. 'These two never get this close to winning,' she said. 'It's a plain dance, and hard to judge. Usually the winners are favorites — it seems like the same ones always win.' She took the names to the judges who had the two ladies dance another round, then they selected the winner. 'Those two were so happy to come in first and second! Everyone was shocked, but happy for them,' your Auntie told me. I motioned her to sit close to me, then I whispered to her what I had discovered. I hadn't scrolled down far enough. The scores went from low to high, and the next page had the top scores. There were a whole bunch of names on that page with higher scores. She looked at me, shocked. 'Do you want to be the one to tell them?' she asked me, pointedly. 'No way, no how, but I will if you want me to.' I answered. 'Close the folder,' she said, and we kept that secret. I never talked about it until this day."

Sam burst out laughing. "Oh my gosh, Becky! I bet those judges were shocked! I wonder if they ever realized what happened?"

Becky declined to come into the house, saying she was tired and needed to get to bed. She thanked them and gave hugs all around. As she drove back to her place, she marveled at the huge changes in her life in this short week.

Becky had poured her life into her career. She married late, and had no children. Her marriage had imploded eleven years before when she discovered her husband had a sexual addiction he wouldn't let go of...something she couldn't live with. A few years later she retired from teaching and moved here to be near Judy and the ocean. She tried to get to the beach for a walk every day. She had read about negative ions coming off the water and being good for one's health. Whatever the reason, she always felt better after a walk along the shore. The things she missed – having family near her and being involved with her indigenous friends – were given back to her in one moment when she ran into Rod that day. He and Sam, and their family, had made her life on the reservation easier. Now maybe she could provide that for them.

CHAPTER TWENTY-THREE

When Jessica got up Sunday morning she went out to the kitchen, Heather resting on her hip, to make herself a cup of tea. Her mother was sitting at the table, talking on her phone. "I don't know what to think. I know she was in that wreck and has amnesia from it. And she had that brain surgery...but would that change her so much? She don't even hug me like she used to." Deloris glanced up, saw Jessica in the doorway, and said, "She's up. I have to go now. Call me later." She put down her cell phone, turned to Jessica, and said, "That was your Pa, checking to see how you are doing."

Jessica handed Heather to Deloris, with her bottle of formula, sat down and wrote.

THIS MUST BE HARD FOR YOU THE TRUTH IS I DON'T KNOW YOU OR WHAT I CALL YOU

"Mama. You call me mama."

While Deloris fed the baby, Jessica took her time, writing carefully, trying to put her feelings into words that would help Deloris understand how this was for her. OK MAMA I HAVE NO MEMORY

THE DOCTOR SAYS IT WILL COME BACK UNTIL THEN I'M STARTING OVER CAN YOU ACCEPT THAT IF NOT IT MIGHT BE BEST IF YOU GO HOME THE STRESS IS TOO MUCH FOR BOTH OF US

"Well now, I must say that's a bit hurtful," Deloris said after reading the message. "But I understand. Your pa also called to tell me that your Granddaddy took a turn for the worse. He's in the hospital, so it would be a good thing for me to go home. If I can get a flight out tomorrow, is there someone who could take me to Olympia, to get the shuttle? Only, I don't want to leave you alone with the baby."

BECKY WILL HELP ME ASK HER TO TAKE YOU

Jessica called Becky and handed the phone to her mom.

"Hello, Becky? This is Deloris, Jessica's mama. I'm calling to see if you could possibly take me to Olympia tomorrow, if I can get a flight change. Her granddaddy is ill and I need to go home. I think she needs me here, though. She says you might help her, but I really think I should stay, and help y'all."

"Of course, Deloris, I can take you if you need me to. Please, put Jessica on."

"But, honey, she can't talk to you!"

"Just put her on, please. We have a signal."

Deloris passed the phone to Jessica. "Hi — listen, if you want your mom to go push a button once, twice for her to stay." Becky heard one beep. Jessica gave her mom the phone.

"Deloris, I can come over and stay with Jessica, no problem. It will make it easier for us to work on her voice. You go home and be with your father. If anything happened to him you would feel awful."

"Well, that is true, dear. Alright, then, I'll get a flight and see what time I need to be at the shuttle, and let you know."

Jessica got on her laptop, opened her mother's flight information and rescheduled for 2:00 the next afternoon. With the time difference she wouldn't get into Louisville until after 9:00 p.m., but a nephew would pick her up. The shuttle would leave Olympia at 9:00 a.m. for the drive to Seattle-Tacoma Airport. Once everything was arranged Deloris called Becky to ask her to pick her up at 7:00 a.m.

Jimmy came out of the bathroom, showered, and needing coffee. Jessica poured him a cup while Deloris explained the situation.

"Are you sure you'll be alright here alone?"

"She won't be alone. That Becky lady said she'll stay here with her until she can get along by herself. That way she can help her start talking again. Maybe she'll start remembering things again. It's something when your own daughter don't know you!"

Jimmy caught Jessica's eye, and winked. "I know how you feel. She doesn't know me either, her own husband! From all I've seen of Becky she'll be fine with Jessica and Heather."

They spent the rest of the day sightseeing. They went for brunch at the Tokeland Hotel, a beautiful restoration from the 1800s, then drove around the reservation. Jimmy took them to Westport to see the boat he would be spending the next few months on, and left his gear there, on his bunk. They had dinner at the Aloha Cafe, the best barbecue any of them had ever eaten.

When they turned in for the night, Jimmy tucked Heather into her crib, which was in their room while Deloris was here. Then he crawled into bed, in his tee shirt and shorts. He had never taken his shirt off in front of her. He had told her he had severe acne on his back and didn't want her to see it. Jessica was on the very edge of the bed, the blanket wrapped tightly around her. He lay watching her sleep. He hadn't tried to touch her, hadn't even hugged her, since they got home. He sensed how fragile she was, and couldn't imagine what it would be like to try to love someone you didn't even recognize. He smiled, remembering all the wonderful lovemaking they had before. Time would heal her, he hoped, and that would be a good memory for her too.

I can feel him watching me. He hasn't tried to touch me since we came home. I don't know what I would do if he did. I wish that wreck had taken away my memories, and that I wasn't faking it. I think I will go crazy if I don't talk to someone about this. But who, how? What do I say...I'm Marie, the dead woman, trapped in the body of the woman who lived, but she really died and her soul went to heaven and left me behind with this incredible mess? I can't tell anyone, because they wouldn't believe me and probably would put me in an asylum. Then who would raise Heather? I can do this. I can.

She slept hard, without remembering her dreams. In the morning, Jimmy left with her mother and Becky, to be dropped off at the boat before they went to Olympia.

Finally, she was alone with Heather. Alone at last, with her baby, who still slept soundly. She peeked in at her, then went to make coffee. Cup in hand, she wandered through the house, looking at the decor, foreign to her, not things she would have picked at all. Who was this Jessica? She found photo albums and a yearbook in the bookshelf.

Thumbing through the yearbook she discovered Jessica had been a majorette in high school. So had she! That was the only thing her mother would let her out of the house to do, twirl her baton. The football and basketball games, the parades, all gave her freedom from that oppressive house. She never dated in high school but was allowed to take part in the band activities.

Jessica was in her junior play. Marie had starred in her senior play, so they had that in common as well.

She found a tablet and started a list. She looked at the photos of Jessica with her brothers, Robby and Patrick. One was a '57 Chevy that Patrick had restored. She added that to the list of things she could talk about, bringing them up as she "regained" her memory. She found their wedding photos. They had been married in a tiny church on the beach in Ocean Shores. She decided to go out there one day, to walk the beach, visit the church, and make her fake memories, to add to the ones Jimmy had shared with her. She was determined to be as prepared as possible for when Jimmy returned, and to make a life with him.

She jumped up and threw the album on the floor. *Who am I kidding??? He is a rapist. He may be a killer. There is no way I can ever have a normal life with him. He's going to come back and they will arrest him and that will be that. I'll have to make a life for Heather and me. But I will not be Jessica Wilson. I'll change my name, and Heather's name. We will move away so he can never find us.*

She picked up the album, put it back in the bookshelf, and went into the bathroom. Looking in the mirror she opened her mouth and began to talk. It came out in a raspy voice, more than a whisper, but not normal, yet. "Hello, there, Jessica Wilson. I'm Marie Harper and I am now taking up space in your body. OMG...I sound like E.T."

Heather woke then, and Jessica spent the next hour getting her bathed, dressed and fed. She sang the mouse song to her, as she fed her, and did the creepy crawly up her arm, both of them laughing as they played this ritual together. Just as she took her out of the highchair, Becky knocked, and let herself in.

"Everything went perfectly! I dropped Jimmy off this morning and swung by the dock just now. The boat is gone. Your mom is something else! She shared with me that she doesn't drive and depends on your dad for everything. She said she had never been out of the county where they live before! She hates flying and will never do it again. She's probably in the plane, ready for take-off by now. How are you doing?"

"Great!" rasped Jessica.

"Good! How would you two like to go to Westport with me to visit my friend Judy? She has invited us to a late lunch after we do a beach walk."

"Sounds good. I'll get my jacket. Is it OK for me to talk this much?"

"Absolutely. Just take it easy, and if it gets sore, or starts to go away again, then rest it. Take the white board just in case."

"Could you get it? It's in the living room on the table."

Becky went over to the coffee table and reached for the whiteboard. There was a tablet on top of it with a list. At the top were two names, Marie and Jessica, with lists underneath. She read several entries and put it down when she heard Jessica coming back. She handed the whiteboard to Jessica, who dropped it in the diaper bag.

What the blazes was I looking at, wondered Becky.

CHAPTER TWENTY-FOUR

Rod spent Monday morning at the Tribal Police office, bringing Chief Winters up to date on the case.

"It sure sounds like you got your man, Sarg. It all fits together without a shred of real evidence."

"I know, right? Everything is circumstantial. But it was enough for a search warrant for Jimmy's house. I had it faxed here. Did it come in yet?"

"Let me check." He called the front desk and it was there. Just then a text came in from Becky. 'If you got that search warrant, now is a good time to go. Jessica and Heather are with me for the afternoon. There is a tablet on the coffee table you need to see. The key is under a flower pot on the back steps.' 'Thanks. I'll go right now.' he texted back.

He grabbed the warrant, said "later," to the Chief, and left for the Wilson's house. He let himself in with the key, and went straight to the living room, where he found the tablet. *Damnation, what is this woman up to?* he wondered. He read and reread the two lists, trying to figure out what they were. *So, we have a woman, Jessica, who can't remember anything, making a list of things from her life, and also from the life of a dead woman she never knew. Why, and how did she get the information?* He looked through the bookshelf, found the yearbook, opened it up and read about Jessica on various pages. The first four items on the list were verbatim from the book. *Maybe she is trying to remember her life this way,* he thought. Looking through the photo albums, he found proof for three more items. *Nice car! OK, maybe this is helping her remember...but what about the Marie list? How does she know this stuff about her? Did Jimmy know this much, and tell her about Marie? Is this the kind of stuff people talk about on a first date? If so, why would he tell Jessica? And why would she make a list, comparing them?* He took a screenshot of the list then put it back.

He went through the house, the truck, garage and the tool shed, carefully, but couldn't find anything to tie Jimmy to the crimes. No cigarettes, no clothesline, black bags, nothing. Since the killings were ritual, and annual, maybe he got rid of the evidence each time. *This is killing me,* he thought. *Nothing makes sense.*

He texted Becky, told her he was finished, and asked her to let him know when they returned so he could come back and tell Jessica about the search. While he waited, he went to the office to make a copy of that list, and think about it a while. As he drove onto the reservation, he thought he saw something out of the corner of his eye, turned, and watched as the form of a woman evaporated into the air next to him. "Shit!" he yelled, and pulled off onto the side of the road. He shut the car off, got out, and stood, shaking, looking at the passenger seat. "What the hell was that?" He walked into the woods, leaned on a tree, closed his eyes and prayed for an answer. As he stood there, supported by a giant fir, he emptied his mind. Suddenly, he saw the counter of the restaurant Jimmy had taken Marie to...saw the four photos of the dead women laid out there...and realized the woman he saw in his car was one of them.

He drove to the station, jumped out of the car, and ran into Chief Winter's office. "Hey, Rod, what the heck is wrong with you?"

"Chief, something happened to me out on the road." He explained what had occurred in his car. "Do you know why she would come to me like that, back from the spirit world?"

Chief Winters had prepared a smudge as he listened, and began cleaning Rod with it. As he swept the smoke around Rod's body, using an eagle feather to move it, he said, "My boy, I have heard from my elders that spirits sometimes try to communicate with us to clear up the mystery surrounding their deaths. I think this young woman was letting you know you are on the right track. You had just come from Wilson's house, right? You didn't find anything. Maybe she was there to tell you to keep looking, but in a different way. Now go, think on it."

CHAPTER TWENTY-FIVE

Back at Judy's, after a walk on the beach and lunch, the three women sat and watched Heather, on the floor, with the dogs. She had one hand curled in Luna's curly poodle hair, and the other was being licked by Beatrice. She laughed every time Bea's tongue wiped over her fingers.

"Becky has told me a bit about what happened to you and Heather. I'm so sorry. And so glad, at the same time, that it ended up like it has. I've never heard anything like this!" said Judy.

"Thank you for caring," Jessica squeaked. "All I want now is to create a normal life for us. Being with the two of you today has been perfect. Both Jimmy and my mom keep waiting for me to remember them, but you two are new to me, and make it so easy!"

"I'll do anything I can to help you," shared Judy. "Babysitting, anything."

"I appreciate that."

Becky read Rod's text and shared, "Rod wants to come over as soon as we get back to your house. I have a bag of my things in the trunk so I can stay over with you, if that's all right."

"Yes, please! I really don't want to be alone right now, until I can take care of everything easily."

Judy questioned her, "How are you doing physically, with everything?"

"My headaches are gone! I have no pain from the hind brain surgery, except my stitches are itching. I've had to pull some of them as they fall out. I've had a few episodes of the throat closing, like the doctor told me I would. It's the strangest sensation, I feel it swell, and then close. I take a big breath when it starts and hold it until it opens again. It's scary."

"It sounds scary! Will that stop?"

Jessica was growing weary and could barely get the next words out. "Dr. Singh says it will diminish with time, and eventually go away."

"It's a good thing Becky is staying with you then. That sounds dangerous."

"You're tired, Jessica, and it looks like Heather is ready for a nap. Let's get you two home." Becky got up, picked up Heather, and Jessica got her bag. They hugged Judy and left.

Becky texted Rod before they got on the road, letting him know they were on their way.

He left the police station and got to the house as they were unpacking the car. He carried Becky's bag in for her.

Becky made coffee and they caught each other up while Jessica put Heather down for her nap. When she finished with the baby, she joined them, and made herself a cup of tea. When the three of them had sat at the table, Rod began.

"Jessica, I have some difficult news. I told you in the hospital that Marie Harper had evidence on her body that led us to conclude she was a victim of that serial killer, and that she got away somehow. We have investigated further and there was enough circumstantial evidence for us to think that because the timing was right, and that Jimmy had sex with her around that time, that he may be the killer."

He waited, watching her reaction. She seemed resigned, as if she wasn't surprised. "A search warrant was issued for this house and I came over while you were out and did a search. I didn't find anything to connect Jimmy to the murders, but we are convinced he is the killer." He paused again, letting the weight of his words sink into her; watched as she slumped in her chair, tears forming in her eyes.

He filled her in on a few details they had, and Becky shared their belief that he had developed DID. She read a bit of the research on that to Jessica.

"Did you ever get him to tell you anything about himself?" Rod asked.

"He told me he grew up in Aberdeen..." She told them the rest of his story.

"None of that is true. I'm going to share with you the truth, because I believe you need to know who you are married to, so you can decide how to handle your relationship with him." He proceeded to tell her the details of Jimmy's early life.

When he finished, Jessica put her head down on the table and cried. *No wonder he has such a nice side, and that awful darkness I saw that night. He doesn't have a twin; he has another side of himself.* Becky grabbed a tissue from the box on the counter and gave it to her. Wiping her eyes she said, "Thank you for telling me, Sergeant Kills On Top. I feel so much better knowing everything. What does that mean for us? I can't take Heather away from here because she is not legally mine."

"We're working on that. You are married to her father. We will talk with Social Services and see what the best way is to proceed. Meanwhile, you need to keep up appearances with Jimmy. Text with him when you hear from him. Keep working with Becky on your voice. I noticed you don't have a drawl..." he smiled.

"No. It seems to have left me. Maybe when the squeak goes away, I'll have it back."

"You could pretend, copy your mother's drawl. It sure is pretty! I bet you could do that, with the acting you did in high school."

"How did you know that?"

"I saw that list you made when I was doing my search. What was that about?"

Oh shit. Her eyes slid from his down to her hands, which were folded in her lap. She started twisting her wedding ring. "I thought if I looked in my yearbook and photo albums it might help me remember. At least it would give me things to talk to Jimmy about... as though I remember. I even planned to go back to where we were married. That was when I thought we could still have a life together."

"I saw that. Very proactive of you! What about Marie's part? How do you know those details?"

"I asked Jimmy to tell me about her, so I could tell Heather. When he told me she was in drama and a majorette, I was shocked."

"I bet you were," said Rod. "When I asked him about Marie, he said he didn't know any details of her life, that they had just been out the one time, and she did not share much, except about where she was from, that she was an only child, and that her dad had died. He didn't know what kind of work she did, which is a usual first date conversation."

She picked up the whiteboard. I'M TIRED CAN WE STOP

"Of course. Go get some rest. Becky and I will visit for a bit."

They went out on the porch and sat in the rocking chairs, with their coffee. "Where are you, deep in those thoughts of yours?" Becky asked.

"She's not telling us all the truth. Something is going on with her. See what you can find out, okay?"

"I agree. She became agitated when you questioned her about Marie. Rod, do you think they did know about the baby, and planned the wreck, hoping it would kill Marie?"

"I've thought of that, but I don't believe so. I think whatever it is, it goes back to what made her afraid when she first saw him, after she woke from surgery. That was an obvious fear. Something happened to make her afraid. And I don't believe whatever it is would have shown up with a memory loss. Becky, I don't think she lost her memory. I think she's faking it."

"Are you serious? Of course, you are. I hadn't thought of that! I'll try to steer our conversations with that in mind," she said.

"Good. Just don't scare her, OK?" He got up, handed her his cup, and left the porch. "Later."

She smiled. "Later, sweet boy."

CHAPTER TWENTY-SIX

Becky had been with Jessica for a week before she felt comfortable bringing it up.

They had settled into a routine with Heather's care and the household chores. The little cottage had a small kitchen with a table for eating, the living room, and two bedrooms, with the bath in between. There was a large, glassed-in porch on the back side, where Becky slept. She loved waking with the sun kissing her face first thing in the morning.

Jessica's voice was back to normal, and they had gone into town for a check-up with the doctor. Both her neck and her hind-brain surgery were healing well.

Social Services had been out to check on Heather and interview Jessica. The paperwork had been filed for her to have custody with Jimmy.

They were sitting out on the porch on a beautiful morning in May. In Washington, that was rare, so whenever the sun was out, so were the people. "This is a lovely teapot," Becky said, as she poured another cup for Jessica.

"Thanks. Jimmy told me it was a wedding gift from a woman I worked with at the restaurant."

"Do you want me to call and let them know you are doing well? Maybe your friend would like to come for a visit."

"I don't think so. I don't remember them, so it might be awkward."

"Your voice came back beautifully...but no drawl. Does that still concern you?"

"No...that's the least of my worries now." She got up and started pacing the length of the porch. Slamming her hand on the railing, she shouted, "I'm trying to figure out how to get out of this marriage without Jimmy knowing." She turned and looked at Becky. "Sorry for the outburst. I've about had it. Honestly, Becky, I've been thinking over everything and there is something I can't get my head around. I totally get why Jimmy killed his mom. What I don't get is why he started killing other women and burning them."

Here we go, Becky thought. She knew Rod had not mentioned the burns to Jessica. That fact had not been released and they had agreed not to tell her.

"My understanding of the alter personality is that sometimes they get fixated on a behavior and it reoccurs, especially on significant anniversaries. This alter of Jimmy is a psychopath and whatever drives him would need to be discovered in therapy, if that is at all possible. Did you ever see Jimmy's back?"

Jessica thought about it. *She's talking about ever, as in our marriage. I have only been in this house with him two days.* "He keeps his tee shirt on, all the time. He shuts the door when he showers. No, I haven't seen his back."

"Jimmy's back is covered with scars from cigarette burns. We're sure it was his mother who did it. When they found her body, she had cigarette burns on her breasts."

Jessica returned to her chair, her face showing the horror she was feeling. "Oh, my God! That's terrible. That's why he burned the women!"

"Jessica, that fact has never been released in the news and Sergeant Kills On Top didn't tell you. How did you find out?"

She looked up, surprised at this question. "He must have told me. I'm sure he did."

"No, he didn't. He kept that fact back when he told you about Jimmy's past. How do you know about that? Whatever it is, don't worry. Just tell me the truth."

So here it is. I finally trapped myself. I'm so tired of living this lie. Can I trust her? Does it matter? Slumped in her rocking chair, her hands raking through her hair, she looked at Becky. "You'll think I'm crazy."

"No, I won't." Becky reassured her. "Nothing you can say will make me think you are crazy. Come on, trust me."

Jessica looked up at the sky, watched a cloud drift away, shook her head and said, "You want the truth? Here it is." She turned and looked Becky directly in the eyes. "I'm not Jessica Wilson...I'm Marie Harper."

She's batshit crazy! Becky sat for a moment, trying to digest this revelation. "What did you say?"

"I said I'm Marie Harper...in Jessica Wilson's body." She got up, and moved to lean against the porch railing, watching Becky as she tried to come to grips with this unfathomable piece of information.

This lady is clearly delusional, thought Becky, watching her, warily. *Something terrible must have happened to her brain to make her think she is really Heather's mother. Some kind of psychotic break. I'll play along, make her think I believe her.* "How is that possible? How can you be Marie, when she died!" Becky exclaimed.

Jessica moved again, this time standing behind the rocking chair, grabbing the back for support. "That night, of the accident...I was standing outside my car, looking in at my body. I was trying to grapple with the fact that I was in two places at once. I had read about what they call out-of-body experiences and thought I was having one of those."

"I've read about those. I've actually known people who had them," replied Becky. "But they are alive. You died."

"Yes, but I didn't know I was dead." Her voice rose and started to shake as she continued. "Then I saw Jimmy get out of his truck and come over to my car. I recognized him. I had dated him once. He raped me and that's when I got pregnant; how Heather was conceived." She started pacing again. "I think he recognized my body too, and when he saw her in the backseat he figured out that Heather might be his. He took her and put her in his truck.

"I was out of my mind with anger, and so afraid for her. I tried to yell at him, but he didn't see me. That's when I knew I had died. I saw his wife's spirit leave her body! She came to the car, looked at me and at Heather, then just vanished. Have you ever heard of that?" she asked.

"No, only in movies. *City of Angels, Ghost.*" Becky smiled.

Standing in front of Becky now, her hands outstretched in front, imploring, she began to sob. "When the paramedics were trying to revive Jessica, I was right there next to her. I prayed that I could stay here, as her. The next thing I knew I woke up in the hospital in her body. I remembered everything from my life. I knew nothing about hers. Honest, Becky. That's what happened. Please, please believe me!" She knelt on the floor then, in front of Becky, rocking herself into a fetal position, sobbing loudly.

"I want to, Jessica, or Marie — but this is a lot to take in. I believe that we have a soul, and that it goes on somewhere else when we die."

Jessica got up, kneeling in front of Becky. "Think about everything!" she screamed. "How I can't remember one thing about Jessica's life. I don't know Jimmy at all, or my supposed mother, for crying out loud! I don't have that friggin' drawl!" She stood and went behind the chair again. She held up her hand and started listing what she knew, her fingers counting the evidence. "I do know Heather and everything about her. I can tell you when she cut her first tooth and had her vaccinations. Get my phone from the police evidence and look at the photos of her. I will tell you what's on there, and where I took them. I can tell you how to process medical records, yet you will find no evidence of Jessica ever studying that...only me, Marie! I will describe to you what I looked like, what clothes I am wearing in the photos, what was in my house, my social security number, anything to make you believe me!" She banged the chair on the porch as if it were punctuation, emphasizing her last thought.

Holy, moly frijoles. Unbelievable! How could she be making this up! Rod thought she was lying about the amnesia, and maybe he was right. It's all so surreal. Becky looked at Jessica, saw the determined look, the change in her face that telling the truth had brought. "Well, if this is all true, it explains a lot! So, you never lost your memory, or your drawl, you never had them to begin with."

"Right! You believe me?" She started to laugh with joy, then to cry again. Becky moved from her chair and crouched next to Jessica, holding her as she sobbed. Relieved at finally telling the truth about what had happened to her, Jessica began to calm herself again. Becky went into the house for a box of tissue, which she gave to her friend, then sat back down on the floor next to her.

"Jimmy burned me with a cigarette. When Rod told me there was a mark the killer left on the bodies, I knew what it was, and I knew Jimmy was the killer. I couldn't tell you because, well, now you know why. I didn't know how to tell you guys who I was without you thinking I was crazy. I was afraid you would lock me up and Jimmy would get Heather."

Becky processed this information, crazy as it seemed. *There is that. She knew about the burns. As preposterous as this sounds, it is the only thing that makes sense. I'm going to believe her until we can prove something different.* She put her arm around Jessica and began to weep herself. "Oh, Sweetie, how terrible for you to have gone through this alone, all of this on top of the crash. I can't fathom what you have gone through. I have to call Rod." When he answered she said, "You need to get over here as soon as possible!"

CHAPTER TWENTY-SEVEN

Ten minutes later Rod was sitting on the couch with a fresh cup of coffee, looking at the two of them. He noticed both had tear-stained faces. "I take it you have something important to tell me?"

Becky started. "Jessica mentioned this morning the cigarette burns on the victims. When I told her she had no way of knowing about the burns, because you hadn't told her, she explained to me how she knew. She has something to tell you. You need to listen to this with an open mind. It explains everything, why she has no memory, why she has no drawl. It's going to be hard for you to believe. I've never heard of anything like it, but I think it's the only plausible explanation for all of our questions. Please hear her out."

"OK...go ahead," Rod said. Jessica proceeded to explain to Rod what she had told Becky, carefully and calmly. Becky watched Rod's face as Jessica slowly revealed each detail of her story. Becky questioned her when necessary for elaboration, to help him understand. He was normally so good at covering his thoughts, his emotions, but this was too much. She almost laughed out loud as his face registered the shock. When his coffee cup tipped in his hand, almost spilling its contents on his lap, she grabbed it and set it on the table.

When Jessica finished, Rod sat back, closed his eyes, and thought... *Occam's Razor, Occam's Razor...what is the definition? In layman's terms, the simplest explanation is often the correct one.* He opened his eyes. "So, you are never going to get your memory back?"

"I have my memory. I don't have Jessica's and I never will."

I have never heard of anything like this. I wish I had my elders here to ask them if they have. This definitely clears up all the questions we've had, he thought. *But what a story. How could they possibly convince a judge or jury?* "Do you believe this, Becky?" he asked, shaking his head.

"At first, no I did not. But as she gave more facts, I couldn't deny the possibility. Can you think of a better explanation? All the questions we had she explained with this scenario. I will believe it until we can disprove it. If we look at everything from this angle, maybe we can solve the crimes. After all, she knew about the burns!"

Rod looked at Jessica pointedly. "Tell me some things about you that most people wouldn't know; things that I can verify."

She scooted forward on her chair and began quickly. "I graduated from Hoquiam High School. My drama teacher was Ms. Anderson. We did Noel Coward's play, Blithe Spirit, and I played the ghost. Funny, huh, considering? I was a National Merit scholar." Rod circled his hand in front of him, encouraging her, "More," he said. She thought for a moment then smiled. "I got called into the principal's office once! I attended a seminar at Seabeck, my senior year. When I returned from that weekend, Principal Campin called me in and asked me about Saturday night. It was Halloween. Some of us had gone to the cemetery to have a seance. He told me some students had been invited by the instructors to a party where they drank alcohol and smoked pot. I had no knowledge of that. He said my story was the same as the others, who had been at the seance, and thanked me for behaving myself! You can call him and check that out, He's still there at the school."

"I have never heard of such a thing as you are describing to us. Of all the known facts that have stumped us from the beginning with you, this unknown phenomenon is the only plausible explanation, as Becky said. I'm going to believe you until there is another explanation. I don't think we need to tell anyone else about this. We can help get you away from Jimmy with everyone thinking you are Jessica." He looked at her, shook his head, and said, "What do you want us to call you?"

They all laughed, which broke the tension. "Jessica is fine, for now. I'm used to it. But I'm choosing another name when this gets finished!"

Rod sat back and closed his eyes again. "I need to ruminate some more on this!"

"Great! Jessica Marie, let's fix us some lunch," said Becky.

CHAPTER TWENTY-EIGHT

Rod sat in the chair, thinking, until lunch was ready. He had made a mental list of what needed to happen now.

When they were at the table, he looked at Jessica. "I can't wrap my mind around this...what you have gone through since the accident. You are an amazing woman, Jessica, to have pulled this off without him suspecting anything. Somehow, we need to figure out a way to enter it into the police logs that you were raped by Jimmy, burned, and got pregnant. This will be enough to get him arrested while we put it together with the evidence from the murders. The restaurant owner remembers you being in there with him. That's one good witness that can identify you with Jimmy. And we have the receipt for the dinner for two the night of the rape. You can't testify as Marie, now, for obvious reasons. We have to find proof. You didn't happen to keep a journal, did you?"

"No. No journal."

"Did you keep the clothes you were wearing?" She shook her head no. He thought, then said, "OK...It's water under the bridge, but I'm wondering why you didn't report it at the time, that you were raped?"

"I called my mom and told her. She said no one would believe that it was a rape, because I went out with him. She told me to just keep it to myself. When I found out I was pregnant, I moved back in with her. I was afraid Jimmy would see me somewhere, and think it was his baby. If I told the police then, and they caught him, he definitely would know. So, I kept my mouth shut. I never wanted to see him again, and I certainly didn't want him near my baby. And look how it all turned out!"

Rod thought again about the coincidences life had thrown in to bring it all out in the open. "By the time we finish this investigation he will be arrested and won't be near either of you again. Have you heard from him?"

"Yes, he put money in our bank account, and we have texted a few times."

Becky had sat listening, then spoke up. "Jessica Marie, think back to that night, before the rape happened. Close your eyes and see yourself getting ready for the date. You were happy to be going out. Did you have anything that you still have, shoes, jewelry, anything that Jimmy might have touched?"

Jessica sat with her eyes closed for a couple of minutes. She saw herself after the rape, crawling around on her living room floor, crying, picking up pearls. Her eyes popped open. "My grandmother's necklace. She had a long, double strand of pearls that she gave to me before she died. I wore it that night. Jimmy choked me with it and it broke, the pearls running all over the floor. Later, I picked them up and put them in a little jar, hoping to get it fixed someday!"

Rod jumped up. "Those should be in the boxes of personal items they removed from your house. I was going to bring them to you to go through and save anything you wanted to give to Heather, in case you choose to tell her about...Marie – your life. They are at the Shoalwater police station. I'll go and get them."

As he drove to the office, he thought about it long and hard, troubled by what he would say to her, not wanting to lead her or ask her to do anything incriminating. He placed the three boxes in the trunk and returned to the house.

He took the boxes in, and gave her an evidence bag and a pair of gloves. "I'm not going to stay here while you do this. Go through the boxes. If you find the jar, place it in this bag, and return it to the box. I will take them back to the station and go through them." He looked at her pointedly. "It's a shame you didn't have a journal or something to connect us with those beads. I'll have to think of a way to let the Chief know why I want to check them for Jimmy's DNA. See you later." and he left.

"I hear Heather waking. I'll get her up," said Becky.

Jessica went through the first box, nothing. In the next box she found the jar. She sat and looked at it, wondering how she could help. Finally, she picked up her tablet and a pen, and wrote: 'My Grandmother Edythe's pearl necklace, broken by James Wilson, the night he raped me, 1/10/2017.' She tore the paper from the tablet and folded it, placing it in with the beads.

An hour later Rod returned, picked up the boxes, and took them back to the station. A few minutes later, he knocked on the Chief's door. "I may have the evidence to solve our case," he said.

Chief Winters beckoned him into the office. "Tell me!"

"I thought I'd go through Marie Harper's belongings to see if there was anything that might help us, you know, a journal or something. I found this." He handed him the jar and a pair of gloves.

Chief Winters put on the gloves, read the note, put it back in the jar, and said, "Send it to be tested, now!"

"Right. I went through all the boxes. There's nothing left that might be useful. Is it okay to take them to Jessica, so she can pick out stuff to save for Heather, when she tells her about her other mother?"

"If there is nothing else that can be considered evidence, sure. Go ahead," the Chief agreed.

Rod went back out to his desk, removed the note, put it in a bag, and placed it in evidence. Then he sent the jar of pearls out for testing. He put the boxes in his car, called Becky and asked her if she would meet him at Washaway Beach.

Becky parked behind his empty car. She looked around, and saw him sitting up on the hill, on a huge tire that had been placed there to keep cars from driving off a road that no longer existed. The old road ended where the ocean had eroded the land. He sat, perched, sixteen feet above the beach, looking out to sea. She could tell by the slump of his shoulders that he was in a bad space in his head. He gave her a hand up, as she climbed to sit beside him on the tire. She waited for him to speak.

"Do you know what I found in that box?"

"No. I was in the bedroom when she went through it."

"Good. The jar of pearls was there, with a note that named Jimmy as the rapist who broke them. It was even dated 1/10/17. I sent the pearls for DNA testing. I didn't send the note, because I don't know if it was written then, or today."

"And you don't need to know. It doesn't matter. Jessica Marie is telling the truth. We know that. Now there is evidence to arrest him, if his DNA is on those pearls."

"I feel like I committed a crime, hinting that she should do something. What if she did write it today?"

"The crime was committed by Jimmy! And there is no way for her to testify in court and get people to believe her. Marie is alive, in Jessica's body, and deserves justice, as do those other women! Let it go, Rod. Be grateful she remembered the pearls, and that you can hopefully use them as evidence to keep him from killing again next January."

He jumped off the tire, yelling, "You're right. I don't know. I don't want to know!" He turned and leaned into the tire, placing his head

140

on his arms. "Let's wait and see what the results are. You know, that doctor said this was at the top of his Strange Happenings list. He had no idea! I still can't wrap my mind around it. It feels like we are all puppets and someone is pulling the strings to get the results they want."

Becky patted his shoulder. "You've been watching too much *Blacklist*! I think it is more like a cosmic event; that we are somehow being helped by a divine being to ferret out the truth and help justice be served. Maybe Jimmy will be helped too, by all this. Perhaps he can get some treatment to make his alter disappear."

"That reminds me...Jessica wrote James Wilson. I've only heard him go by Jimmy."

"That could be critical, Rod! When an alter takes another name the initial personality usually doesn't know about the alter. That would help Jimmy in his defense."

"It would also help us, potentially in contacting James. By calling him that, being tough with him, he might come out."

"Why would you want to do that?"

"We have to, to prove the alter is there. If Jimmy doesn't know about James, and we arrest him, Jimmy's not going to know what we are talking about. We need to confront James on tape, then show Jimmy, after a psychologist explains to him what has happened to him."

"That makes sense. Do you want to come back to the house and ask her about the James thing? I have a pot of chili for dinner."

"That's a good idea...and I'm hungry!"

They climbed down off the tire and Becky walked over to a rusty, iron sculpture someone had created, a man in a fedora holding a camera. In the middle of the camera, was a hole, perfect for one to place their own camera to take a photo of the beach. "This is creative! What is this place anyway?" she asked.

"Washaway Beach, they call it now. There used to be a town down there. It was settled in the late 1800s. Gradually it was taken by the ocean, clear up into the 1970s. People couldn't save their homes because the government forbade them to build anything to protect them. See that house over there on the hill, with the berms around it? That guy went ahead and spent a ton of money to build that wall around his property. His house is still standing."

"Wouldn't it have been easier to spend that ton of money to buy another place?"

"Maybe. But, for him, it was the principle of the thing. It's his land and if he wanted to protect it, he should have the right to do so. Come over here and see what I found once, down on the beach." They walked over to the other tire. There was a corroded machine on it. It was filled with a conglomeration of seashells, rocks, and sand, making a kind of cement filling throughout the machine.

"Is that a VCR for showing movies?" Becky looked at it, incredulously.

"Sure is! The first VCR was made in 1975, so this was in a house that went into the bay after that. It washed up on the beach one day, like a lot of other mementos. People have found all kinds of things."

"That is so creepy!"

"Yeah", he said, looking at her with a sly smile, "I always imagine those houses down there...ghost houses, with the tables still set."

"Geez, Rod, that is dark! Let's go eat!"

CHAPTER TWENTY-NINE

While Becky made cornbread using P.J.'s recipe, Rod talked with Jessica. "I don't want you to tell me anything about that note except to answer questions I ask. Understand?" She nodded. "I noticed you wrote James on the note, and not Jimmy. Why is that?"

"When I met him in the store he went by James. At least that's how he introduced himself when he asked me out."

"What was his personality like then?"

"Cocky, really sure of himself. At dinner he was arrogant. I was glad I had my own car and left right after we finished eating."

"Did you ever see the Jimmy we all know?"

"No, never."

"Did you touch the jar, the pearls, or the note with your bare hands?"

"No, I wore the gloves that you left."

"One more question. Did James say anything to you during the attack?"

She sat quietly, then looked up at him, tears filling her eyes. "He called me a whore. When he was burning me, he said, "From your little bastard.""

After they ate, Rod helped clean up while Jessica was with the baby.

As Becky swiped a sponge over a plate, swishing it through the soapy water, she said, "Rod, I just thought of something. I noticed Jessica is left-handed and her writing is tilted. I'm not asking what the writing in the jar looked like, but I'm wondering if it might be a good idea to have her go through her boxes and get rid of any writing that might be in there."

"I love the way you think! I can't ask her to do that, but I can look. This makes me wonder about a lot of things," he said, as Jessica joined them.

"What does?" Jessica asked as she made herself a cup of tea.

"Well...for starters what hand did you use when you were Marie?"

"Both. I wrote and ate with my left and did most everything else with my right."

"Everything else, like what?"

"Use my mouse, bowl, pitch a ball, golf, knit, and twirl my baton. Why?"

"You are eating left-handed now too. Is your handwriting the same as it was before?"

"Yeah, I guess so. I hadn't thought about it."

"This is fascinating. Do you still feel like you are the same person as when you were just Marie? Have you changed at all?"

"I think I'm braver, more confident. That could be because of what I've been through, right?"

"We don't know. Would you please ask Jessica's mom next time you talk to her what hand you used to write and eat?"

"Oh, you are wondering if Jessica is left-handed. That would be a problem, wouldn't it, if Jimmy noticed something so obviously different?"

"You could just blame it on all the brain stuff, like everything else! Is he on his way to Alaska?"

"No, I think they are still berthed in Blaine for another week."

Right then the door opened and in walked Jimmy.

"Surprise! We finished getting the boat ready, and got a couple of days off, so I rode back down with a guy from Westport."

He walked over and picked up Heather, giving her a kiss on the head. "I missed my girls! So, your voice must be back. I saw you talking through the window."

Becky recovered from the shock of his appearance first. "Welcome back! Yes, she has been working very hard. Before she says anything, I want to let you know she had a seizure or something while she was incapacitated because she has no drawl. The Pacific Northwest inflection is predominant now. Sorry, Jimmy."

"Well, at least you can talk. Let's hear it!"

Jessica said, "This IS a surprise. I'm glad you could come home for a few days. Heather started to walk holding my hands this week and now you can see that. Put her on the floor and sit in front of her. Hold her hands to help her stand and she'll come to you."

He sat Heather on the floor. "That's a mighty pretty voice your mom has!" He noticed the boxes stacked next to the couch. "What are those boxes?"

"I brought those by," explained Rod. "It's a few of Marie Harper's personal things that we thought you and Jessica might want to go through and keep some for Heather."

Jimmy looked at the boxes, straightened, turned toward Rod, and said stiffly, "No! Get that stuff out of here. I don't want it in my house. Heather doesn't need any of that. That's in the past!" Then he quietly began to play with Heather, coaxing her to come to him.

Becky and Rod exchanged glances then stood up. "Jessica, since Jimmy is home, I should go back to my place. Call me when you want me to come back."

"OK. Thanks for everything you have done."

"You are very welcome," Becky answered with a hug. She went into the sunporch and gathered her things while Rod carried the boxes

145

to his car. Jessica followed her in and whispered, "Did you hear him? That voice he used...he sounded like the James part of him!"

"I did! Keep your phone on you and call 911 if you see any evidence of him fronting again. I'll talk to Rod about it," and she left.

Before they had reached their cars Jimmy was out on the porch, calling, "Wait! I changed my mind. Please bring the boxes back. I wasn't thinking straight. Of course, we might want some of Marie's things for Heather." Rod took the boxes back to the porch. Jimmy grabbed them and took them inside.

CHAPTER TWENTY-NINE

Rod and Becky got in their separate cars and headed toward the reservation. Rod pulled into the Roadside Cafe, Becky followed, and he invited her in for coffee. As soon as they were seated and had ordered, he said, "Hey! Did we just get a glimpse of James?"

"I think we did. I was hesitant to leave Jessica Marie with him after he got angry. She mentioned it and I told her to call 911 if she got frightened of him. It looked like he transformed back into Jimmy quickly, though, when he was playing with Heather."

The server brought their coffee and pie, lemon meringue for her, and coconut cream for him.

"Becky, I have a question about James and Jimmy. If James is the alter, and Jimmy doesn't know about him, how does Jimmy know about Marie? I'm thinking back to that first conversation I had with him, when he told me they had dated. He told me about her and their conversation over dinner. She described him with the James personality, and says she didn't ever see Jimmy. How is that even possible?"

She put her fork down and sat staring at her pie. "We missed it, Rod! There must be another alter, one who knows the other two... maybe Jimmy doesn't know about either one. The other two know each other."

"That would explain it! I remember that article you sent me said the patients with DID usually can't remember what each alter does when another one is fronting...fronting means coming out or taking over, right?"

"Yes. It also said that some of them can talk to the other alters. Maybe James and #3 communicate. Just now, when James exploded, the one who came out to get the boxes must be the third one. James protects Jimmy, and #3 cleans up after him! He makes things OK for Jimmy, after James acts out. He protects them both! What is the first time we know James showed himself?" asked Becky.

"When he killed his mother."

"Right! And after he killed her, he covered her with his coat. That's not something a person in that kind of rage would do. I think #3 covered her with the coat."

"And it must have been #3 who went over to Marie's car, saw her body, and made the connection. He took Heather to keep her safe. He had the conversation with me at the hospital! Becky, will you come back with me to the station, so we can make a chart of all this? Honestly, I'm so confused I don't know whether to scratch my watch or wind my butt!"

She laughed at him." That's one of my favorite lines from the play, *Steel Magnolias!*"

"Yeah...it was one of my mom's favorite movies. She made me watch it with her so many times one winter when there was three feet of snow and it was twenty-five degrees below! I feel we are in over our heads, and need some expert help, but I don't want to introduce anyone new into Jessica's life. Jimmy coming home threw a wrench in our nice, clean plan to solve this while he is gone. We don't want him to get suspicious and stay." They got up, he paid the bill, and she followed him back to the station, where he introduced her to Chief Winters.

The Chief, a large, burly man with two gray braids, shook her hand and said, "We are pleased, ma'am, that you have helped us so much with this case. Thank you."

"You're welcome, sir. I'm very happy to be of assistance. Is that a Gary Hillaire painting on the wall?" asked Becky.

"Yes, it is. I bought it from him years ago, at a powwow, before he went to the spirit world. You know his work?"

"Yes. He was a friend of mine. We belonged to the same Faith."

"You're a Baha'i, then?"

"Yes, Chief Winters, I am. How do you know what Baha'i is?"

"Several years ago, one of our young men came back after going to college in your world. He had joined the Baha'i Faith. He started a group for youth here on the reservation. They study together about the world's problems and do service projects. Almost every teen is in his group. He has shared your Faith's teachings about indigenous people, and the role we will have in bringing about a just and peaceful society. Families love him and what he stands for."

"I am so happy to hear that! Youth empowerment is part of the model we have for community building. Now, I'd love to share with you a story about Gary Hillaire. He was like a brother to me. It was his nephew, actually, who first told me of the Faith, when he was a student in my second-grade class, in 1971. Gary came to see me, and gave me a book of Baha'i Scriptures. A few years later, I visited Gary's family on the Lummi Nation.

He had just begun to do those air brush paintings like you have there. I commissioned him to do one for me, of a large butterfly, with my favorite colors. When he brought it to my house he hung it on the wall, stood back looking at it, and began laughing that great laugh he had. I asked what was so funny. 'That's one of a kind,' he told me, 'and someday, maybe, it will be worth a lot more than you paid for it.' 'Why is that?' I asked him.' Because my little girl tore up the template for the butterfly. There will never be another one like it!'" They all laughed at that.

"I didn't see that butterfly in your house," Rod said.

"No, I gave it to a Persian friend, who loved it. She had left Iran, in the '70s, after the Shah was deposed, and the persecutions of the Baha'is began. She had lost family over there, and I wanted to give her some joy. She has left this world, now too, and I have no idea where the painting is. Someone is enjoying its beauty, I'm sure."

Chief Winters looked at her with compassion, went over to the wall, and took down his painting. He held it out to her. "My people know about persecution. Please take this in honor and memory of Gary Hillaire and your Persian friend." Becky held her hands out to him, and back, three times, then placed them around his gift. She had learned this way, of accepting something given, from her Hidatsa friends. She said thank you in his language. "Hiyu masí…I will treasure this for the rest of my life."

CHAPTER THIRTY

Rod and Becky went to the conference room and cleaned off a whiteboard. Becky picked up three markers, and wrote Jimmy, James and #3, each with a different color. They proceeded brainstorming, listing everything they could think of under each name that would support the idea of three different personalities. That's when they started to think that the dominant personality was #3, and that he was Jimmy. They came to the realization that the real Jimmy Wilson, the little boy who had been brutally tortured and raped, who didn't make friends or communicate well with anyone in the group home, had withdrawn from the world, and the two alters had taken over, to protect the child within.

"I'm astounded! This is the only way everything fits," exclaimed Becky. "He's in there, somewhere, and has no idea his life was railroaded by these other two."

Rod took the files on Jimmy out of the cabinet and opened the earliest one. He read through each transcript slowly, looking for something in a conversation he had seen between Jimmy and his therapist. After several pages, he found it. "Skip! That's what his nickname was. Listen to this from his therapy notes:

"Therapist: Jimmy, you went to Head Start. The teacher there said they called you Skip, that you chose that name because there was already a Jimmy and a James in your class. Why did you choose Skip?

Jimmy: The neighbor has a dog named Skip. I like that dog.

Therapist: Would you like me to call you Skip?

Jimmy: No! Don't ever call me that. Call me Jimmy."

"That poor little boy! By the time he was ten Jimmy had taken over. That would explain how he changed through his teen years, became more confident, held down a job, finished school," mused Becky.

"We need help. I have no idea what to do here." They went back into the Chief's office and shared with him what they now believed to have happened.

"Rod, I think you are right. And I agree you need to bring someone else in on this. As soon as the results come in on those pearls, if there is evidence that he is the killer, we need to make an arrest. But who are we arresting? There is a psychiatrist working for the Skokomish tribe who might know how to handle this, Dr. Stephanie Bowstring. She has worked with all the police forces in Mason County over the years. Let me get in touch with them to see if we can borrow her. Meanwhile, stay away from Jimmy while he's home this week. You don't want to scare him. I'll see if I can get a rush on that DNA test."

As they walked out to their cars, Rod got a text from Sam. "She says to come to dinner. P.J. already has the rocks in the fire. She said you can use one of her dresses for the sweat. And she has blueberries for you to make wojapi!"

Becky got out of her car at Sam's and went to stand with P.J., by the fire, warming her backside. The sun was just setting and a chill had replaced the afternoon sun. "Thank you, P.J. for doing this for us. I have nothing to give you today, as thanks, because I didn't know I was coming."

"Hey, no problemo! Sam said you are making wojapi. I can't wait to taste it! That's enough, thanks."

"OK then, I'll go do that!"

She put the berries in a pan and added enough water to go about halfway up the berries. She mixed honey with a little flour and added it to the berries as it cooked, stirring all the while. Finally, it had thickened, and she poured it into bowls for everyone, keeping some back for the spirit plate. She added that to the portion of beef stew P.J. had brought and the fry bread Sam had made, poured some ice tea into a cup, and took the two containers out and placed them on the top of the sweat lodge. "For all my relations," she said.

"Chief Winters told us that the kid who is working with the youth is a Bahá'i," Rod shared over dinner.

"That's what you are, innit, Becky?" Sam said. "I remember that from back home. I remember my folks laughing when Smokey said the only people who showed up at the Catholic church to wrap the Christmas presents for the kids in town were the Bahá'is. Hey, Becky... someone started a rumor that you killed Brother John," she laughed.

"Good grief, no! He did come over for a cup of tea the week we moved to Mandaree. He told us he didn't want us to try to influence his flock with our beliefs. I assured him that isn't our way, that we don't proselytize our Faith. Then, from what I heard, he went home and died."

"What?" P.J. yelled. "For reals?"

"Unfortunately, yes. It was rather bad timing."

They all laughed, until P.J. snorted tea out his nose, which sent them into more gales of laughter. "I wonder what happened when he got to heaven and found out that he was wrong...that our way, your way, all ways are paths back to the Creator?" asked P.J.

"Amen," said Rod. "The rocks are ready. Let's go into the lodge now, and clean up later."

The four rounds went by quickly, with a short break between each one so people could go out, get cooled off in the fresh night air, and have a drink of water. During the prayer round Becky thought about the situation they were in with Jessica Marie and Jimmy, and prayed, "O Lord! Protect us from what lieth in front of us and behind us, above our heads, on our right, on our left, below our feet and every other side to which we are exposed. Verily, Thy protection over all things is unfailing."

Later, as they were cleaning up the kitchen, Rod said, "That prayer you prayed. It sounded similar to one Uncle Garland used to say in the lodge back home."

"That one is in the Baha'i Prayer Book. I believe it's similar for the reason P.J. alluded to: that all spiritual paths are connected. The Creator sends the Holy Spirit through different messengers at different times in history, to bring teachings to humanity for its next stage of development; the essential spiritual message is the same."

Sam interjected, "That part about unfailing protection. That's not true. Look at all the horrible things people do to each other. Why does the Creator let that happen?"

Becky answered, "I can only give you my thoughts on it...I have no direct line to the Creator!" They laughed.

"I think, out of God's love for us, He gave us free will. We mess up. We make bad choices. Sometimes those affect others. I think when something bad happens, like an accident or illness that takes us young, maybe if that person had lived something much worse would have happened. I think life is like that oil lamp you have there, Sam. It's lit now, and burning brightly. If you leave it there, it will burn down until the oil is gone, and it will extinguish itself.

"If the window is open, and a breeze comes in and blows it out it's over too soon. In life, if you make it to the natural end, you're like the lamp that burns itself out; hopefully you have learned what you need to know, and have lived a good life here on this earth. If you are taken early, by illness, an accident, or God forbid, a purposeful human action, then you are like the lamp the wind blew out — finished too soon. He is unfailing in His protection. I think, when we leave here before our appointed time, we receive whatever we need in the next realm from the Creator, as compensation. And remember — God is forgiving. If humans were perfect, what would there be to forgive? Those are just my thoughts about what I've learned."

"That's good stuff. I never thought about it that way, eh? Thank you, Becky."

"You are very welcome, dear girl. Now, I need to get home before I drop!"

CHAPTER THIRTY-ONE

Jimmy played with Heather until it was time for her to eat. While Jessica fed her, he went through the boxes.

Jessica watched him carefully. He is relentless, she thought, going through each box carefully, sorting out items that might be saved for Heather, and a pile to toss. As he sorted, she imagined him evaluating whether anything could incriminate him. He picked up a notebook she had kept poetry in, some by her favorite poets, Dickinson, Mary Oliver, Yeats, e.e.cummings, Maya Angelou, Neruda, and others. She had been writing poetry for years and hers were in the notebook, as well.

Jimmy sat reading, then said, "Marie wrote poetry, Jessie. She's a good writer. I hope Heather will take after her that way. Listen to this one."

He read aloud:

> Requiem to the Trees
> Tall you are, majestic.
> Waltzing in the wind

you caress me as I pass under
your lowing branches.
Cedar boughs swish air
like gentle hugs
from a whispering angel.
Tree hugger I am
depending on your strength
and a place to lean
my weary head.
Tucked into you
my face against
your bark I
contemplate;
thank you for your
green gentleness
and for the dance -
always for the dance.

Marie 2016

"We should keep that book, Jimmy, for her," said Jessica.

He reached up to put it on the coffee table and knocked Jessica's tablet to the floor. He picked it up and saw Marie's name on it, and hers, and the lists.

"What is this?"

"I was looking at my yearbook to see if I could remember anything and I found my high school play, and that I was a majorette! I started a list to see if it would help me remember. I went online and looked up Marie's yearbook from Hoquiam and learned that she was also in drama and a majorette. I want to know things about her to tell Heather."

"What's this about Ocean Shores, where we got married?"

"I thought I would go over there to see if it jogs my memory. I want to remember, Jimmy, I do!"

He got up and brought the tablet and the notebook to the table, sat beside her, and pointed to the writing in each one. "This is almost identical."

"Jimmy, do you know which hand I use to write?"

"Yeah, you are left-handed. Why, don't you know which hand you use?"

"I do, but I wanted to make sure I was that way before the accident. So much has changed with this memory loss. Do you think Marie could have been left-handed? That would explain why the writing is similar."

"I guess. You're right, you've changed a lot. Honestly, Jessie, you don't seem like the same person. Your personality is different — your mom noticed it too."

"I know it's been hard on you, but I am doing the best I can to heal from everything."

"I'm sorry for putting pressure on you, Jessie. Why don't we go over to Ocean Shores tomorrow and I'll show you where we got married? You liked the shops there. We can go to the Casino for lunch."

That sounds nice. I'll ask Judy if she can babysit Heather."

"Who is Judy?"

"A friend of Becky. She lives at the condos in Westport."

"Should we be leaving her with strangers?"

"They're not strangers, I know them. And it's better than her going to a casino! Besides, we need this time to ourselves. I'll call her, ok?"

"Yeah, go ahead." He smiled at the thought of her wanting time with him alone.

She called Judy and made arrangements to drop Heather off in the morning.

As she got ready for bed, she looked at herself in the mirror. She still reacted to this new face every time she saw it.

She had read an article about people who had heart transplants, and how they sometimes changed afterward; how they liked different foods, and activities. It said one lady all of a sudden wanted to ride motorcycles. Later she met the family of the young man who had died, whose heart she got, and learned he was a biker, and loved cheeseburgers, her new favorite food!

I had a whole-body transplant. My mind is the same, but this body is totally different. I need to keep a list of things I find are different about me!

She picked up the hand mirror and checked the back of her head. They had shaved a portion where they had taken out a piece of her skull, about the size of a fifty-cent piece. Her hair was shoulder length, sculpted in the back, and covered the spot, thankfully. Dr. Singh had told her that they couldn't put a patch where the piece of skull had been removed. There wasn't room. Her brain needed the space. He had returned her scalp without any protective covering over the brain. She touched it, carefully, and felt the soft spot. The doctor had told her not to let anyone stab her there! What a weird thing to say, but she understood the warning. Any damage there could hurt her brain. The scar where they had opened the lamina over the first three vertebrae was healing nicely.

When she looked up, Jimmy was watching her. He came into the bathroom, picked up her Vitamin E oil, poured a bit into one hand, turned her around with the other, and gently rubbed the scar with it. She looked at him, in the mirror, really looked...she saw his face for the first time, not as the man who had violated her, but the man who cared so deeply for this woman she was now. He wasn't handsome, in the classical sense. His eyes were beautiful, a dark, turquoise blue.

His beard and mustache he kept trimmed short. His hair, yellowish brown, the color of the grasses in the dunes in fall after they had lost their greenish summer hue, wavy, just brushed his collar. "Do you ever shave your beard?"

"No, I've had it for years. I had acne really bad as a teenager, and the beard covers most of the scars. See, we both have scars," he grinned.

Yes, we surely do. And yours go so deep they may never be able to heal. "Is that why you don't take your tee shirt off at night?"

"Oh, right. You don't remember that either. Yes, that's why. I'm uncomfortable having anyone see my back."

He had rubbed all of the oil into her neck. She realized this was the first time he had touched her skin since she was here, as Jessica. She turned and faced him. "I know it has to be difficult for you, having had a loving relationship with me and then having me treat you like a stranger. How long did it take me to fall in love with you?"

He chuckled. Taking her hand, "Come on, I'll tuck you in and tell you that part of our story."

He stacked the pillows up, so she could sit in bed comfortably. He lay across the foot of the bed, on his side, head propped on his elbow. "You were the aggressor, right from the start. I told you about how you asked me to Thanksgiving dinner, and then we started dating. I had never been in a real relationship before. I had dated, but nothing serious. You made life so much fun, and so easy, that I fell for you quickly. I have a hard time trusting women, for a lot of complicated reasons. But I had been observing you for months at the restaurant. You were everybody's friend, yet you kept a distance with the guys. I admired that. When you asked me to dinner I was totally knocked for a loop. I was like, in a trance, for days before Thanksgiving. That began our "courtship" you called it. It never got physical before we married. You were adamant about that, Jessie.

"You told me you had boyfriends you went to bed with, and it always ended badly. You were determined to not repeat the pattern. You decided you would get to know the next guy you dated without the physical part and see what happened. We only hung out for three months, but by that time we knew we wanted it to be permanent. I proposed on February first. So, I guess by then you were in love with me! So, what's that? A bit more than two months?"

"So, we never had sex before we were married. You respected my wishes? That's wonderful."

"Jessie, for the first time in my life I feel secure. You are my safe place, my home."

"What happened to you that made you feel unsafe?"

She watched as the struggle took over his face until finally it had a set determination and his eyes clouded over. "Don't worry...don't tell me if you are uncomfortable. I don't need to know."

He rolled onto his back, staring at the ceiling. "Thank you. It's past. Let's leave it there."

"I can do that. Can you give me two months, like before, to love you?"

He flipped on his side again, and grinned at her. "Does that include the time I'm gone fishing, or does it start when I get back?"

"You're going to be gone for two months! How can I grow to love you while you are absent?"

"Well, maybe I shouldn't go."

"No, you need to do this. You want to do this. My memory might come back while you're gone. Whatever, I will work on it!"

"Can I at least hold you while we sleep?" He looked so pathetic, she burst out laughing, which made his face droop even more.

"I'm sorry...can you JUST hold me?"

"Yes, ma'am, I promise."

"All right, then. I trust you to keep your word," she said grinning at him.

She pulled his pillow from behind her, put it next to hers and turned on her side. He turned the light off and got in beside her, slowly, until he was snug against her, his arm curling over her waist. She put her hand on his. *This is so weird. I feel like I'm in one of those old Twilight Zone TV shows where everything seems normal but it's not. You're watching and waiting, just knowing the boogeyman is going to scare you out of your skin when you least expect it. Are you going to turn into the boogeyman again, Jimmy?*

CHAPTER THIRTY-TWO

The next day Rod called Becky to see if she was available to go to Shelton with him, to the Skokomish Tribal Center, and see Stephanie Bowstring, the psychiatrist.

"I was going to help Judy watch the baby while the kids take a day off. Let me check and see if she can manage by herself." She texted Judy, got the go ahead, and told him she could be ready in half an hour.

When Rod picked her up, he told her that he had already spoken on the phone with Dr. Bowstring and given her most of the details of the case. She asked that they come in so she could go over a plan with them on how to handle the arrest if there were to be one.

Dr. Bowstring shook their hands as they introduced themselves. "Call me Stephanie. This is a fascinating case," she said. "You have two people presenting with rare personality issues. I'd like to talk about the woman first. Let's go get a cup of coffee and go into the conference room."

When they had made themselves comfortable, she began.

"In the 1970s, Ruth Montgomery wrote a book, *STRANGERS AMONG US*, about people who were not born into their bodies but took over someone else's body when they died. They are called 'walk-ins.' Believers in this phenomenon maintain that it is possible for the original soul of a human to leave a person's body and for another soul to 'walk-in.' In Montgomery's work, souls are said to "walk-in" during a period of intense personal problems on the part of the departing soul, or during or because of an accident or trauma. However, these souls have not lived on earth before, and they retain the memories of the person they are replacing.

"Your case here is different, with Marie leaving her own body and becoming one with Jessica, and keeping her own memories, and not Jessica's.

"I treated another patient, a woman, several years ago who had an unsettling paranormal experience that drove her to see me. It was along this line, but different. I want to tell you about it because it has similarities to Marie's experience, in that the walk-in didn't have the memories of the person he replaced. My patient has since died, but I saved the tape of her talking about the experience." She pushed the button on the recorder, and they all listened intently as the patient described a bizarre incident.

"*Dr. Bowstring, I have been in a kind of shock ever since this thing happened to me. I hope you can help me understand it. I was packing up my things, as we were moving. I had boxes of books all over the living room. Our house had sold but needed a pest inspection and I called for one. The inspector arrived, did his work, then came into the house with his report. He looked at a book I had in a box, NEW CHOICES IN NATURAL HEALING, and asked me "Who is healing in this house?" I told him it was me, that I had been diagnosed with fibromyalgia, and was looking into alternative treatments.*

"*He closed his eyes for a moment, and when he opened them he said, 'I'm supposed to tell you my story.' He told me that he was not always in human form, that he had come from where we call heaven. His work was to greet humans when they died, and to hear their stories. He said that he began to wish to have a human experience, to live life on earth, create his own stories. He asked for the chance to live among us. His wish was granted.*

"He said there was a man in a hospital in Portland, Oregon, who died of a heart attack. This spirit who came from heaven took over the dying man's body. He said that when he woke up in the hospital, he didn't know anything about the man. He had to learn everything. He said his wife knew within days that he was different and asked what had happened to her husband. I asked if he told his wife, ever, and he said no, he hadn't. He told me about a woman he kept from committing suicide, and other events in his life. Then he asked if he could help me with my healing. He said he couldn't affect my physical being, but that he could help me in other ways. He stood in front of me, with one hand in front of my forehead, and the other in front of my heart. I felt this incredible energy flow through me, and he said that I would be in balance, emotionally and spiritually, for the rest of my life. Dr. Bowstring, I don't know if he was real or not. I wonder if he was crazy, or am I crazy for even believing in the possibility. That's why I'm here. Am I crazy?" Stephanie shut the recorder off, and they contemplated what they had just heard.

"Dang," said Rod. "I've never heard of this kind of thing!"

"I know, but that doesn't mean it isn't real. As indigenous people, you and I know a lot about the spirit world that other cultures don't experience or believe. Isn't it possible that there are spiritual experiences we don't know about?" asked Stephanie. "This woman, Jessica, knows things about Marie that she couldn't possibly know...the most important one being the cigarette burns on Marie's breasts. I think you have to believe that she is Marie!"

"What about you, Becky? Have you ever heard of this?" asked Rod.

Becky nodded. "I read Montgomery's book. She thought Abraham Lincoln was a walk-in! I don't know what to think. I believe that there are mystical experiences that happen to people. I haven't read anything in scriptures that would validate this...but I haven't read anything that would negate it, either. I believe this is the only physical experience we get in the material world, our life here on earth, and that there are spiritual realms beyond this. I have no idea if or how they interact with each other. It's all a mystery to me!"

Rod left the room to answer his phone. When he came back, he said, "The DNA results are in. James did touch those pearls. We need to talk about how to approach him. I haven't the slightest idea."

"Has anyone seen the Skip personality that you are aware of?" asked Stephanie.

"Not that we know. Is that important?"

"It might be. If the alters are always fronting, Skip may not be aware of them at all. When we work with people with DID our focus is on integrating the parts of the personality back together. They don't have multiple personalities — they have no personality, just these fragments. Obviously, James came out to protect Skip from remembering the abuse. When he was working at the store that night he was Jimmy. Seeing his mother triggered James to front and kill her. Jimmy remembers what James does, and vice versa, or his life wouldn't be so orderly. It seems like Jimmy is the main alter who keeps everything together, am I right?"

"That's the way we see it. So how do you think I should approach him?" asked Rod.

"Is there any way you can get him to come to the station, so you are not alone with him? Maybe call Jessica and tell her you need to talk to both of them about something you have learned about Marie and Heather. You could have the video running. It might be a good idea if I were there to talk to him," advised Stephanie.

"Yes, I agree!" He called Chief Dolan, in Aberdeen, and filled her in on Stephanie's assessment, and asked if she could be in the interview with Jimmy. Dolan told him that the paperwork for the adoption was ready. She said she would ask Social Services to have it delivered to the police station for Jessica and Jimmy to sign. She gave permission for Dr. Bowstring to be there. The three of them sat down to strategize the meeting where they would confront Jimmy/James.

CHAPTER THIRTY-THREE

Jessica and Jimmy had spent the day at Ocean Shores, looking through the museum and browsing in shops. They walked on the beach and Jessica found a few agates. Afterward they went to the chapel where they had been married. Jimmy walked her down the aisle to the front and stood with her, holding her hands. "We wrote our own vows," he told her, then recited them from memory. "I, Jimmy, take you, Jessica, to be my wife. I will love you more each day as we make our life together. I promise to protect you and our children, to make our home a safe haven. As long as we live, Jessica, I am yours." Her eyes filled with tears as she thought about the meaning behind his words. He had promised the woman he loved a different life from the one he had as a child. She couldn't help herself. She gently took him in her arms and held him for a moment.

At the casino they went through the lunch buffet, and Jimmy watched as Jessica loaded her plate with several seafood selections, and some vegetables, placing each portion carefully so they didn't touch. She had separate smaller plates for salad and bread. At the table she ate from each portion, slowly chewing until it was gone, then going to the next food on the plate, always in a clockwise circle. Once around, she took a bite of salad, then bread, then began again.

It was like deja vu for James. *What the hell is she doing? I've seen someone eat like that before but not her...where...who?* He watched her, thinking, trying to remember.

"Do you always eat like that, keeping your food from touching, eating in a circle around the plate?" asked Jimmy.

"Oh, I started this when I was a kid, at the dinner table. My folks fought a lot and it made me nervous. I calmed myself this way." she shared quietly.

"Hey! You remembered something! That's great! I can't imagine your sweet mother fighting with anyone." he said. "Are you nervous now?"

Holy crap! I just talked about my real parents, my story. I have to be careful! "Not so much nervous, but I guess I'm worried...about my memory not totally coming back. What will we do if it doesn't?"

"Don't worry. You can't control it. We will deal with whatever happens."

Her cell phone rang, and she answered. She listened as Becky explained that they needed to stop at the police station in Aberdeen on the way back. "The DNA came back positive. You need to be extra careful not to reveal anything to him. We may need you to tell him who you really are in the meeting. Just tell Jimmy that we have the paperwork for the pending adoption."

She hung up, looking at him excitedly. "Jimmy! They have the paperwork for the adoption ready for us to sign. We need to go by the police station in Aberdeen on our way home."

"It's a good thing I haven't left for Alaska yet," Jimmy said. "This is perfect. We'll get the papers signed before I leave."

You may not be going to Alaska, she thought. She called Judy to let her know they might be late picking up Heather.

"No problem. Becky called and filled me in. Hang in there, kid!"

At the police station they were shown into an interrogation room where Sergeant Kills On Top, Becky, and another woman were sitting. Rod introduced Dr. Bowstring to them as a social worker, and offered coffee and tea.

Dr. Bowstring presented the adoption papers for them to sign. When they finished everyone congratulated Jessica.

"Jimmy, there is another matter we need to discuss," said Rod. "When I brought the boxes of Marie and Heather's personal items to your place, I kept one item that I thought might help me with a case I've been working on." He reached into his briefcase and brought out an evidence bag that held the jar of pearls. He handed it to Jimmy. "Before you open this, you should know that it has already been sent for DNA testing and we have the results."

Jimmy looked at him quizzically, then opened the bag and pulled out the jar, which he opened. "Read the note, Jimmy," said Rod.

Jimmy opened the note, read it, and his face crumpled. *What the hell is that?* James thought, and came to the front.

He sat up straight and stared at Rod, his face hard and angry. "You had no right to go through those boxes. I have no idea what game you're playing or why this was there."

"I had every right. I had a warrant to search your home too, which I did. This isn't a game, James. It's a murder investigation that began several years ago. It involves you and Jessica because the autopsy done on Marie showed evidence that she had possibly been raped by the serial killer I was investigating."

James turned on Jessica. "You let them search our house? You knew about this? I trusted you!"

James, calm down. You must let me handle this. You are going to get us in more trouble, thought Jimmy.

Shut up, Jimmy. This is my problem, and I will take care of it.

"What evidence do you have and why do you think it involves me...and why did you call me James?" he asked.

Rod nodded to Stephanie to take over.

"He called you James because we've come to believe that's the part of you that committed these crimes," stated Stephanie. "Jimmy, I hope you are listening because we need you both to be here and help us through this."

"I'm not listening to any more of this crap! Come on, Jessie, we're out of here!" He picked up the adoption papers and started to leave.

Rod was on his feet and at the door first. "Jimmy...you need to convince James to sit down and listen to what we have to say. We are not here to harm you. We want to help. But you have to cooperate. If you don't, I have enough evidence to arrest you, and you'll go to jail without any chance of help."

Jimmy fronted and argued, *Please, sit down, James. Let's listen. We are both responsible for all that has happened...you for what you did to protect us, and me for letting you get away with it.*

He sat down, and Rod took the papers from him. "Please listen to Dr. Bowstring. She is not just a social worker. She is a psychiatrist who has read your case file from childhood. Also, Jessica is aware of its contents, as well."

James glared at Jessica, questioningly. She looked him in the eyes, lovingly, and said, "I will tell you my part, after she finishes, but you must let Jimmy be in control. I trust him."

James, please, I can do this! They are not going to harm us. Let's listen, please? Jimmy begged.

James sat back, closed his eyes, and when he opened them, Jimmy looked at Jessica sorrowfully.

Dr. Bowstring began. "I want you to know that I respect so much the way you have managed to survive the horrible things that happened to you as a child. No one has the right to do to a child what was done to you. You had no way to cope except to split apart your personality to protect the injured child. That's Skip, isn't it, the little boy inside who is so terribly wounded?" Jimmy nodded.

"We have gone through all the files from when you were put into care at the juvenile home. We know about the abuse you suffered. We know you went through your teen years blacking out, not remembering things that happened; and finally, we know about the night you saw your mother again. All of these behaviors are symptoms of a mental/emotional disorder caused by your traumatic childhood. You had no control of what happened to you, or how you responded, Jimmy.

Your mind separated itself into compartments to keep you safe. James became the protector, and you became the one who keeps your life together, on track. You clean up after James. You both protect Skip. Am I right?" He nodded again.

Rod took over. "You were triggered, that night at the store, when you saw your mother and James became the dominant personality. You had no memory, Jimmy, when you returned to the group home, of what happened with your mother that night. When did you remember?"

"I didn't even know about James. I was so confused about that night. First, I just remembered being in the alley, watching myself. I started to have dreams and one night I woke up screaming because I saw myself put my coat over her, my rope belt was around her neck...I saw what I had done, but I didn't remember it! James started talking to me, telling me it was not me, it was him, and that now everything would be OK, because she was gone."

Rod interjected, "I imagine you never heard from James again, until the next January 10th. Were you aware when he took over again?"

"No...not until after, just like with mom. I had no control. I couldn't stop him. I was so scared. It kept happening every year. Sometimes he comes out if he thinks I'm in trouble too."

That is enough! You were so scared, huh, you little crybaby. "This is all a bunch of BS." James said in a menacing voice. "You can't prove

173

any of this. You don't have any evidence from those murders, or you would have arrested me before this. Those pearls and that note could have been fabricated. I think you took my DNA from the house and planted it on those beads!"

CHAPTER THIRTY-FIVE

Rod looked at Jessica Marie. "You need to tell him what happened and who you really are."

"They didn't do anything, James." she said. "I saved those pearls after you choked me with the necklace and broke it. I put them in that jar and I wrote the note."

"What are you talking about, Jessie — YOU did it? You're Jessica, not Marie. How would you know anything that happened to her?"

"I'll explain it, but you need to let Jimmy back out. I'm not telling you anything."

Jessica Marie watched as his face softened and knew Jimmy had fronted.

"I'm here, Jessie. James can hear you, but I'll do the talking now, right, James?"

Reaching over, she took Jimmy's hand, took a deep breath and began.

"Do you remember the night of the accident; you got out of your truck and came around to check on me? You thought I was dead. You bent over with your hands on your knees, crying. Then you walked over to Marie's car, saw her, and took her baby. I was dead, Jimmy. I died that night."

"How do you know about that if you were dead? How could you be dead then and not now?" he asked her.

She turned to him, took his other hand, and held both in hers. "Something happened that night that I can't explain, something extraordinary, a miracle, Jimmy." She proceeded to tell him about the events that allowed her soul to leave Marie and become one with Jessica. She went through the following weeks, giving details to support her story, up until today, in the casino when she was eating.

James popped out, pulling his hands away. "That's what I saw — you were eating just like Marie did, the night we had dinner — sorting your food and eating it in order!"

"Yes! I have had to be so careful to try to cover up my "Marie" self, so you didn't suspect."

Jimmy surfaced again. "That must have been terrible for you, waking up in the hospital finding out you were married to me."

"It was, but I just kept holding onto the fact that I was given this chance to keep being Heather's mother. When we learned that I would have died from cancer soon, I was grateful for this opportunity to be Jessica, a second chance to raise Heather."

Rod took over again. "We started putting it together during Marie's autopsy. The cigarette burns on her chest made me realize she was probably a victim of the rapist but hadn't been killed."

"Why didn't you kill me?" she asked.

"You were begging James not to rape you. You said you could get pregnant. I made him stop. I always wanted a baby."

Jimmy put his head in his hands and started to weep. "I'm so sorry...so sorry... for you, the others, all of it."

Jessica Marie put her hand on his shoulder, and rubbed gently, until he stopped crying.

Dr. Bowstring gave him some tissue, and said, "You have this disorder, which we can prove in court, Jimmy, if you cooperate. Rod will explain it to you."

Rod read him his rights and explained what would happen if he plead guilty under an insanity plea. His case would be heard by a judge, who in all probability would sentence him to a psychiatric facility. He would receive care from a psychiatrist who specializes in personality disorders, with the intent to integrate his parts into one.

"If I do this, if I become whole again, I'll be able to get out and make a life with Jessie and Heather, right?"

Becky watched Rod struggle with his emotions as he answered. "Jimmy, even though you are mentally ill, you have to pay society for what you have done. If you are ever competent to stand trial, that will happen. If it goes to a jury, you will probably be sentenced."

Jimmy stood up, nodding his head, his eyes focused on the table. *Oh my God,* thought Becky. *James is fronting.*

As quickly as she thought it, James grabbed the pen from the table with one hand and pulled Jessica up with the other. He held her in front of him with the pen at the back of her head.

Just as quickly, Rod had pulled his gun and trained it on them.

"Put the gun down, Sergeant," ordered James. "I have this pen poked into the spot where Jessica has no skull. One shove and it's in her brain. I don't know what this part of the brain controls, and I don't think you want to find out. Put the gun down and let us leave."

Rod watched him, dispassionately, wondering if he could get a shot off without wounding Jessica.

"Please, Detective," begged Jessica. "Do as he says. Let us leave. Don't let my baby be without her mother again." Jessica flinched as James pushed the pen further into her skin. "Now! Put the gun down!" he ordered.

Rod carefully reached out to the table and placed the gun on it.

"Pick up the gun, Jessica, and aim it at him." ordered James. Jessica did as she was told, her eyes filling with tears. "Now put it in my hand," James instructed, as he let go of her and reached out for it.

Rod saw the look on her face change from fear to a calm certainty, as she decided to turn and shoot James. "Don't do it, Jessica! Don't become a killer and leave your baby alone." He watched her as she thought it over, then put the gun in James's hand.

"Here's how this is going to go. You call out front and let them know we are leaving," demanded James. "The detective walks in front. We follow. You ladies come behind us. We walk out to the car, and we leave. I should have killed her that night, and I swear I will if you try to interfere with me getting away."

Rod called the Chief, told her the situation, and asked her to clear the front. As they left the room, Jessica looked at Becky and whispered, "Take care of Heather."

CHAPTER THIRTY-SIX

As they got in the car, James told Rod to handcuff Jessica's wrists in front and put the seatbelt through her handcuffed arms. "Don't try to follow us. I will kill her if you do." He drove off with Jessica.

Rod ran back into the station and found Chief Dolan giving instructions to notify state patrol, the sheriff, and all local police departments of the car's description. She told them not to engage, but to call the station to notify them of the whereabouts of the car.

"Kills On Top, you take Officer Sandoval, in an unmarked car, and follow them. Keep your distance and we will let you know where they are spotted. I think he will head toward Olympia, where he can blend in. If he heads up the coast it will be too easy to spot him. We must keep Jessica from harm until we can get to him safely."

As Stephanie left, she said, "Jessica has a good understanding of how he operates. If she stays calm, maybe she can encourage Jimmy to front. If that happens, she has a chance. If not, well, I'm afraid for her. He'll keep her as long as she is an asset, but when he no longer needs her..."

"It's my fault," worried Rod. "If I hadn't told him the truth about his future, he might not have switched, and we wouldn't be in this mess."

"Believe me, Sergeant, there is no way he would have let you take him into custody. He's smart enough to know what happens to killers," said Stephanie.

Rod gave Becky his car keys as he and Carmen got in an unmarked police car. They had just received a call that James's car was spotted on the highway leaving Aberdeen, toward Olympia.

"Thank you, dear Lord, that they didn't try to pick up Heather," mumbled Becky as she drove away in Rod's car. She had called Judy as soon as James had pulled out, telling her what had happened, and asking her to leave with Heather to keep her safe. Judy said they would go to her friend's condo, in another building, and asked Becky to call when she got there.

Becky stopped at Jessica's and picked up clothes, food, and the playpen to take to her house. When she got to the condos, she called Judy. "I'm here, at your place. You can come back now."

Heather was hungry, so Becky sat in the rocker, and gave her the bottle Judy prepared. She stroked Heather's cheek, wondering what would happen to her if this turned out horribly. Then she put her down for a nap.

The two friends went out onto the little patio and sat, drinking herbal tea. It was late. Soon it would be twilight, and the full moon was rising over the lighthouse. In a few hours it would be directly over the ocean, moonbeams creating a ladder across the water, from the horizon to the shore. It would beckon anyone who dared to walk out on the shiny path and collect the prize, a giant opalescent pearl.

A car pulled up, startling them. "It's just me," shouted Sam as she got out. "Rod called me and told me what happened. Geez, Becky, this could go down real bad! He wants me to take you and the baby back to our place in case they come back here to get Heather."

Becky introduced Judy. "She's been my friend for years, Sam, and we are safe here."

"No, I think Samantha is right," said Judy. "Jimmy knows where I live, and maybe where you do too. The reservation is best. As soon as she wakes up, I think you should go."

They sat drinking their tea, and Sam sipped her cola she had brought with her. "Auntie...is it ok if I call you that?" she asked Becky.

"Of course! I would be honored!" she replied.

"Auntie, I've been thinking a lot about this guy and what happened to him when he was little. Terrible things were done to him that made him the way he is. What I don't understand is why this happens out here in your world and not on the reservation. I mean, we have crime, and people do bad things, but I never heard of anyone splitting themselves apart over it. I've been crying over this, Auntie, it just makes me so sad."

Judy looked at Becky. "She's right, you know. In all my years in Mexico and Guatemala I never saw this kind of behavior in any of the communities. What is it about indigenous people that makes them different?"

Backy mulled it over, then answered. "You just said it, I think. Or at least part of it. Community. The reservation is a community of people who have similar values based on their belief system. When I lived with Sam's people, I saw the destruction that years of domination by the greater society had done to them. There is alcoholism, drug use, child neglect and abuse. But when I talked with the elders, they said it wasn't that way before, in their grandparent's day. It started when the children were taken from them and put in schools off the reservation. They were made to change their names, speak English, and wear nontraditional clothing. They were beaten if they spoke their language and used like slaves to work in the gardens and at the school. Many of them, girls and boys, were raped repeatedly. They came back to the reservation broken in spirit, and many didn't survive because they started using alcohol and drugs to escape the pain. They became abusers themselves sometimes. The ones who became strong again had family who helped them heal, and they clung to their spiritual values."

"That makes sense, Auntie. The other thing that helps us is our belief that everything is related to each other. We use nature to heal; the earth, the plants, and animals all have meaning to us. Everything is connected. That's community too. I think in your world you don't have that."

"Out of the mouths of babes," said Judy. "You are wise for your years, Sam. I hear Heather waking. Time for you all to get out of here! I have a salmon I bought down at the docks. Why don't you take it with you for your supper?"

"You come." offered Sam. "Bring the salmon and have dinner with us. We can have a sweat first, just for women. We need to go to the lodge to pray for Rod and Jessica. And for my uncle Ben. I didn't tell Rod yet, but our uncle passed to the spirit world today."

Becky hugged her and said, "I'm sorry, sweetie. He was a good man. He always made me laugh with his stories. What will we do with Heather?"

"My friend Laurie, P.J.'s wife, lives across the street from me. She has three kids, and said she would help with Heather if we needed it."

"I'm so sorry for your loss," said Judy, as she hugged Sam. "I have never been in the sweat lodge. What do I wear?"

Becky thought, then said, "Let's leave Rod's car here, so if Jimmy tries looking for us, he won't spot the car on the reservation. Judy, you bring your car, and Heather and I will ride with you. We'll stop at my place to pick up dresses for the lodge."

CHAPTER THIRTY-SEVEN

While Becky and Judy fixed the salmon, some baked beans, biscuits, and a coleslaw salad, Sam called P.J. to get the rocks in the fire, and three women friends to come for the sweat. Then, while she made fresh iced tea, she told them about her uncle.

"My relationship with my uncle Ben was comical and odd. He was my favorite uncle. He always had me do his shopping. One day we went once to Minot to get his headlight fixed in his truck. The day was going good until we went to the car wash by KFC. His damn sunroof wasn't closed all the way. I was the lucky one, sure enough got dumped on. I was covered in rainbow foam and rainX. The crew that wipes down your windows just stared at me 'cause I was all foamy and wet. My hair was all sticky and stiff. That big jerk told them it was my monthly bath day. We stopped in Makoti to grab Fat Boy's donuts and tea, where I ended up losing his debit card on top of it. He cussed me out all the way to Parshall. Before he brought me home, I kept asking him 'Do you still love me uncle?' 'No, you cold evil witch, you're bad luck!' He was just laughing at me while

I scraped myself off his seat. Geez, I'm sure going to miss him. I'm thankful for all the times I did get to spend with him."

They laughed as she related her story. When the food was ready she prepared a plate to put on top of the lodge.

Judy, watching her, asked, "Why do you do that, put food out for the spirits? Do they really eat it?"

Sam smiled, thoughtfully. "I asked my grandfather the same thing when I was little. He said, 'No, my girl...they eat the spirit of the food!' I guess it's sort of like you guys leaving cookies out for Santa Claus!"

It was pitch black outside by the time they went in. Sam ran the sweat. She sprinkled cedar over the rocks and touched a sweetgrass braid to a rock until it caught fire. She shook it until it was just glowing, then she passed it around for each woman to use to smudge. Each thing she did she described for Judy, as she was new to this ceremony. She drummed and sang to the four directions, and to call the ancestors.

Judy sat and watched the rocks until the glow died off, leaving them in a darkness that was comforting and strange. She could feel the warmth increase as Sam poured water over the rocks, the steam rising and falling over her, like a shower of hot mist.

After that round, and a time to cool off outside, was the healing round. Sam explained that she was going to tell the story of White Buffalo Calf Woman, and then sing her song.

"Pte Cincala Ska Wakan, this is Dances in the Air, way down here. Please hear me as I tell these women how you came to the people to help us heal.

"Before the appearance of the White Buffalo Calf Woman, the First People honored the Great Spirit. But for the Sioux, the coming of White Buffalo Calf Woman brought a most important instrument, the pipe, which is now used in all ceremonies.

"The sacred pipe came into being many, many years ago. Two men of the Sioux tribe were hunting when they saw someone approaching. As the figure grew close, they saw a maiden, in white buckskin,

carrying a bundle wrapped in buffalo hide. As she walked slowly toward them, she sang out and repeated: "Behold me. For in a sacred manner I am walking."

"One of the men had evil thoughts about this maiden. The other man tried to restrain him, but the evil warrior pushed the good warrior away. A cloud descended and surrounded the evil one. When it lifted, his body was a skeleton being devoured by worms, symbolizing that one who has evil in their hearts may be destroyed by their own actions.

"The good warrior knelt in fear as the maiden approached. She spoke to him, telling him not to be afraid, to return to his people and prepare them for her coming. The warrior did so, and the maiden appeared. She said: 'In this bundle is a sacred pipe, which must always be treated in a holy way. No impure man or woman should ever see it. With this sacred pipe you will send your voices to Wakan Tanka, the Great Spirit, Creator of all, your Father and Grandfather. With this sacred pipe you will walk upon the Earth, which is your Grandmother and Mother. All your steps should be holy.'

"She instructed them in the use of the pipe. The Sioux begged the woman to stay among them. They promised to build a fine lodge and let her select a warrior to provide for her, but she declined their offer. Her sacred bundle was left with the people. 'The Creator above, the Great Spirit, is happy with you, the grandchildren. You have listened well to my teachings. Now I must return to the spirit world.'

"She walked away from them and sat down. When she arose, she had become a white buffalo calf. She walked farther, bowed to the four quarters of the universe, and then disappeared into the distance. To this day, a Sioux family, the 'Keepers of the Sacred Bundle,' still guards the bundle and its contents on one of the Sioux reservations."

As Sam completed the story, she hit the drum, and began to sing, "Wakan Tanka, Toka Heya...Becky and the others joined in, as Judy listened, mesmerized by the plaintive, beautifully mysterious song.

After the song each woman prayed from her heart for healing for someone they loved.

Becky asked, "Creator of all, please hear me as I ask you to enter the heart of James and turn him over to Jimmy. He is a pitiful creature who was denied a good beginning by his circumstances. Please help him remember who he truly is, your child. Please care for Jessica and keep her safe until she is back with us. Please help Rod, guide him as he follows them, and keep him safe in his work. All my relations."

When the last round ended, they went out to the fire. Sam loaded her pipe with pure tobacco and drew a breath of the smoke into her lungs, letting it out to carry her prayers. She passed it, and each woman did the same. Then they left the world of spirit, entering back into the material world.

CHAPTER THIRTY-EIGHT

Rod had been following the path James and Jessica had traveled for over two hours, obsessing about what he could have done differently to keep it from going down this way. State patrol and the sheriff had kept them updated on the whereabouts of James's car. It was obvious now that they were headed for the ferry from Bremerton to Seattle. Rod had his lights on, but no siren as he sped down the two-lane road heading into Bremerton.

He was sure James would make the 9:00 p.m. ferry, according to the police reports. Rod knew he would not make it in time, and would have to wait for the next ferry, which meant James would be across before Rod even left this side of Puget Sound. He had a Kitsap County sheriff on the phone who was watching the ferry line. James's car was in the third row. The sheriff watched as James and Jessica got out of the car and walked over to the restrooms. James had put his jacket over her shoulders, covering her arms and hands, which told Rod she was still handcuffed. The sheriff said James had his arm around her, the other at her side. He considered trying to apprehend

187

James while Jessica was in the bathroom, but James went in with her. They exited together a few minutes later and went back to the car, just as the first row started to drive onto the ferry.

Rod got a call just then from Vici, at the Kitsap Transit office. The sheriff had notified her of their dilemma. Instead of them waiting for the next ferry, she offered to send a captain to take Rod and Carmen across on the passenger ferry which would put them in Seattle just minutes after the 9:00 o'clock ferry arrived. She asked if she should notify the captain of the ferry James would be on, and he said, "Yes, please let him know, and that the sheriff will be on the ferry in an unmarked car. Please instruct the captain not to let his crew know anything until the ferry has left the dock, and to stay away from that car. I don't think they will get out of the car." He thanked her, then called the Seattle police to arrange for an unmarked car to meet him when the ferry docked so they could continue the pursuit.

Back in the car, after using the restroom, James did Jessica's seatbelt, making it impossible for her to escape. He followed the truck in front of him and, as directed by the deck hand, drove up the ramp to the second level. They had not spoken the entire trip, until Jessica had said she had to use the bathroom. Now they sat, silent, in the dark.

How can I get Jimmy to come out, Jessica Marie wondered, as she sat trembling. *If I can get him to listen, maybe he can convince James to let me go. I cannot die like this after all I've been through. Please, God, help me figure out what to do.*

The boat continued filling with cars. It would be an hour's journey, and most of the passengers left their cars to go up on top to the lounge.

The ferry pulled slowly away from the terminal and began its journey across the bay, engines chugging loudly, evenly...and the lights dimmed.

James was furious that it had all fallen apart like this. He preferred to stay in the background, letting Jimmy run the show and live his

life without interference. *How could I have been so stupid to let him get involved, get married? If he hadn't, we would not be in this mess.*

We would not be in this mess, Jimmy retorted, *if you hadn't done those terrible things in the first place!*

There was no problem until you wanted me to leave Marie alive, in case she had a baby! Now look at us! You got the baby, you got Marie back, and now we're on the run! James argued.

We were always on the run, Jimmy thought. *Ever since you killed mom, we have been on the run. Every year we're more on the run. I'm tired of it. I'm tired of you.*

Leave me alone! I have to think this through! An hour! I have an hour to make it easier for me to escape.

Jessica sat quietly, in the dark, her hands trying to find the seat belt latch, hoping she would have time to get it undone and the door open before he could stop her. If she could just get out of the car and down the ramp, she would be safe.

James drummed his fingernails on the steering wheel as he thought about the best way for him to get out of this predicament. He got out of the car, went around to Jessica's side, opened the door, and unhooked her seatbelt, letting it slide free from the handcuffs. "Get out!" He put the jacket over her shoulders and started walking her back down the ramp, past the empty cars.

"What are you doing?" she asked.

"Never mind."

What are you doing??? screamed Jimmy inside his head.

What I should have done a year and a half ago and you stay out of it! answered James.

Jessica looked at his face, the anger and hatred pronounced, and she felt the fear from that first night return. *He's going to kill me,* she thought. She pleaded with him, "Jimmy, please hear me! Don't let him do this. Stop him!" *Dammit, I don't have anything to gag her with!* In an act of desperation James pulled off his tee shirt and pushed it in

189

her mouth just as they got to the bottom of the ramp and headed to the aft ferry deck. Behind the last row of cars was a chain, stretched across the ferry, about two feet above the planked floor. Beyond that were a few feet of decking. The dark, cold water roiled behind the ferry as it moved steadily across the bay.

James shoved Jessica down onto her knees, rolling her under the chain as he stepped over it. She kicked the chain up with her foot, catching him in the crotch. He screamed, tumbled over the chain, and fell on top of her. She pulled the shirt out of her mouth, grabbed his face with both hands and yelled, "Jimmy, my love, look at me! For Heather, for me, with all your soul, fight him!"

With every ounce of determination, Jimmy fought to the front, grappling desperately in his mind with James. He opened his eyes and looked at her. "Forgive me, Marie," he said, as he rolled off her and into the frigid water. The ferry continued its run as the churning sea pulled him down into its icy depths.

Jessica Marie lay, weeping, on the deck until people coming back to their car saw her and went for help.

"Lord, help her, she has handcuffs on!" said a deck hand as they helped her to her feet, then took her to their break room where they bandaged a cut on her forehead and wrapped her in a clean blanket.

By the time the ferry had unloaded and was reloading Rod was there. He took the handcuffs off, then helped her to the passenger ferry, where they sat inside, on a bench, and he held her as she cried. He rocked her gently, back and forth, until she was finished.

"It's all over, brave woman. I'm going to adopt you and that's what I'll call you. Your spirit name will be Brave Woman!"

"I don't want you to adopt me," she said.

"No?"

"No. Sam can...but not you!" and she smiled at him lovingly.

CHAPTER THIRTY-NINE

Becky was sitting on a huge driftwood log that had washed up on the beach. Someone had taken a chain saw to it, carving it to look like a raging bull. *That's what this month has felt like,* she thought. *Like a bull, let loose in our lives, and we couldn't get away from it; chasing, until it was breathing down our backs and Jessie Marie finally took it by the horns and threw it down.*

Becky and Jessie had a long phone conversation earlier that morning. Jessie Marie had decided to keep that name...Jessie in honor of the woman who had lost her life, whose body was Marie's salvation; and her own name, all that she had left of who she used to be. She wasn't keeping Wilson, though. She was changing it to Logan, the last name of one of Jessica's grandmother's maiden aunts, from Kentucky.

"I called Deloris, and told her Jimmy died in a fishing accident," explained Jessie Marie. "I told her I'm staying out here, and that she is welcome to visit if she ever wants, but that my memory did not come back, that I'm not the same person she knew. I told her I want

to change my last name and asked her about family history. That's how I got Logan. She was pleased that I asked her."

Jessie had moved onto the reservation, into a small house near Sam and Rod. She was working again for the tribe and had applied to do coding for the medical office in Aberdeen where she had worked as Marie. Sam had given her a great recommendation.

When Becky asked her how she had made these decisions, she said, "The night of the wreck, I was distracted by the sign at the Yoga Studio, 'Kind people are my kinda people.' Reading that sign cost me my life...and brought the kindest people I have ever known into it. You all have shown Heather and me extraordinary kindnesses. I have family now, real family, for the first time in my life. I love you all and want to stay here and have you be part of our lives. Heather will have aunties and uncles, and two wonderful grandmas! I have a second chance at an incredible life with my daughter."

She's right, Becky thought. *We have become a family, through choice. We have our families of origin, whatever they may be, and we have created this family through love. It gives us all a second chance to make a life together in that love.*

"Hey, you!" Becky looked up and saw Rod coming across the sand. "I stopped at your house, then came over to Judy's. She said you were down here. How are you doing?"

She scooted over on the log so he could sit down with her. "I'm okay. Still sad over Jimmy. I know he didn't 'pay his dues' to society, but he sure did to Jessie Marie by keeping James from killing her. He took his life in an heroic act. Do you think that will help his soul in the next world?"

"Yeah, I do. The Creator loves all his children. He made us good. Sometimes what happens to us in life makes the bad come out in us. We leave this world with the best we are and go on from there. Where I don't know. But I believe it's like a circle. The Creator sends our soul out into this world, and we travel through it, learning, living,

hopefully doing some good, until it's time for us to complete the circle, go back to Him.

"That's lovely." Becky answered wistfully.

Rod continued. "And we can always depend on St. Peter. Did you hear what happened when Frankenstein got to the pearly gates? St. Peter said, 'Well, the thing is, only parts of you can get into heaven. How do you want to handle that?'"

Becky burst out laughing. "That is certainly apropos! Jimmy handled it well, I think. His best part stepped up in the end. So, you've completed the paperwork on your cases and things have calmed down. Now what?"

"I'm thinking of going home to North Dakota for a month, to see my mom and grandmother, and take part in the Sun Dance."

"Well, don't be gone too long. You might lose your chance."

"My chance at what?"

"Not what...who! Jessie Marie moved onto the rez and I've seen the way the guys look at her! I've also seen that she only has eyes for you. And I saw you watching her the other night, too, after the sweat when we said good-bye to Jimmy."

He looked at her. "Ya think?"

"Yeah, I think! Seriously, Rod. She and that baby are the sweetest little family and there is room for you there. For reals, as P.J. would say!" They both laughed, and then she pointed down the beach. "Look!"

A bald eagle had left the roost and soared slowly up the beach, its shadow casting wide over the sand. It seemed split apart, the shadow from the bird, but it was one in reality.

As it reached them it did a lazy circle over their heads, flapped its wings, and headed east. Becky felt a whisper of air pass her face. She looked down. An eagle feather lay across her lap.

ACKNOWLEDGMENTS

I want to acknowledge writers of every book I've ever read, from Margaret Wise Brown's *Good Night Moon* to Jo Jo Moyes's *The Giver of Stars*, and the thousands in between. One cannot become a writer without being a reader. Fine literature seeps into one's being and becomes the blood that drives the heart to create with words.

A thousand thanks to the team at When Words Count. If Agent Steve Eisner hadn't read my manuscript and invited me to participate with the other Fabulous Four authors, I may not have had the courage to proceed to a publisher. Thanks to my coach extraordinaire, Gregory Norris, and Peg Moran, wonderful editor who loved my story first! Publicist, Steve Rohr, and Producer, Marilyn Atlas gave great input that helped make this a better book. Andrea Mosier, Lorraine Cover, and Flo Knight – what a supportive, creative team of authors I had the joy to work with!

Dave LeGere and the publishing team at Woodhall Press gave insightful feedback and made the process of moving from writer to author a meaningful and enjoyable experience. Meg, thank you for sharing with me what moved you in the story, as well as what needed more emphasis.

From the beginning, during a long Covid winter, my friend Curt DuBois, my sister Vici McDonald, and my cousin Jan Chapman were with me online, and on the phone, reading, questioning, editing until I had the first edition. Your love and encouragement made the hard moments bearable and the rest of it so much fun! Then my beach buddies, Judy Serrano, and Karen Berg read and offered more insight.

Thanks to Shannon, proprietor of The Yoga Studio in Georgetown Kentucky, for the great first line of my book — "Kind people are my kinda people"; to Lina Zeine, Professor Emeritus of Communication Sciences and Disorders, at Western Washington University, for

information on throat injury and voice disorders; to Don Duncan for his valuable knowledge about detective work; author Christopher Buck for his astute comments and book cover blurb; and Tobi Buckman, childhood friend and psychiatrist, for her critical reading of the novel and comments on my treatment of Dissociative Identity Disorder. Steve Allen, thank you for your feedback, and the wonderful afternoon on the Lummi Reservation where we sat next to the totem pole in the shade of a cedar, as I read to Voir Hillaire the part about his father, Gary. To Patrick, Ed, Will, Evert, and Barbara for your support – bless you! To my daughters, Sarah and Jeannie, with all the love in my heart, thank you.

Finally, thanks to the people of Mandaree, North Dakota, who shared their lives, love, and laughter with me; To Eldora, my co-teacher, my dear friend, who gave me so much support as I learned the customs of the people, and helped me prepare for the Sun Dance; and to Good Road, my Hidatsa friend who never let me pass in the hall at school without making me laugh; who helped me through the worst of times; and who was there as I participated in many of the ceremonies included in this story, always, always love.

While many of the experiences in this book are based on real events, except for Gary Hillaire, Artist, the characters are all fictional.

ABOUT THE AUTHOR

Jenn Chapman drew on experiences with people in her inner circle who had serious personality/character disorders to create the serial killer character in this thriller. Jenn is a retired educator who spent several years during her teaching career working with indigenous populations in Washington State and North Dakota. Reservation life gave her a look into a unique way of viewing the world through a spiritual lens. That led to creating some of the characters in this book; a way to share her love for the people who adopted her and taught her their ways. Jenn loved the inclusion of the tribal elders in the preschool educational program and decided to create intergenerational programs in the wider society using that model. She wrote *Quality Care: An Intergenerational Approach.* She partnered with an architect, Dyke Turner, to start Bridgings, Inc, where they designed and oversaw the building of several intergenerational programs, ultimately receiving an award from Generations United. Their programs were showcased in newspapers, magazines, on newscasts and Good Morning America. She currently lives in Georgetown, Kentucky, where she is writing a second novel based on reservation stories, and working on a modern historical novel about her years living in Guatemala during their civil war. For over fifty years she has been a member of the Baha'i Faith, which promotes human rights, social justice, and the oneness of humanity.